RAVES FOR cut

"*Cut*, a debut novel by Patricia McCormick, is one of the best young-adult novels in years. . . . Riveting and hopeful, sweet, heartbreaking."
—*Boston Globe*

Ms. Emily

"A vivid and inspiring first novel . . . *Cut* is deft and fascinating—part psychological mystery story (what's eating Callie?) and part adolescent drama (will her friends help her get better?)."　　　—*The New York Times Book Review*

★"Callie's first-person account of her stay at Sea Pines, a mental-health facility, is poignant and compelling reading. . . . Shelley Stoehr's *Crosses* (Bantam, 1991) and Steven Levenkron's *Luckiest Girl in the World* (Viking, 1995) dealt with cutting, but *Cut* takes the issue one step further—to help teens find solutions to problems."　　　—*School Library Journal*, starred review

★"First-timer McCormick tackles a side of mental illness that is rarely seen in young-adult literature in a believable and sensitive manner. . . . A thoughtful look at teenage mental illness and recovery."　　　—*Kirkus Reviews*, starred review

★"This novel, like Laurie Halse Anderson's *Speak*, sympathetically and authentically renders the difficulties of giving voice to a very real sense of harm and powerlessness. Refusing to sensationalize her subject matter, McCormick steers past the confines of the problem-novel genre with her persuasive view of the teenage experience."　　　—*Publishers Weekly*, starred review

Patricia McCormick

PUSH

SCHOLASTIC INC.

NEW YORK   TORONTO   LONDON   AUCKLAND
SYDNEY   MEXICO CITY   NEW DELHI   HONG KONG

ISBN 978-0-545-29079-1

All rights reserved. Published by PUSH, an imprint of Scholastic Inc., 557 Broadway, New York, NY 10012, by arrangement with Boyds Mills Press, Inc. SCHOLASTIC, PUSH, and associated logos are trademarks and/or registered trademarks of Scholastic Inc.

12   16/0

Printed in the U.S.A.   40
This edition first printing, May 2011

For Meaghan

I

———————

you say it's up to me to do the talking. You lean forward, place a box of tissues in front of me, and your black leather chair groans like a living thing. Like the cow it used to be before somebody killed it and turned it into a chair in a shrink's office in a loony bin.

Your stockinged legs make a shushing sound as you cross them. "Can you remember how it started?" you say.

I remember exactly.

It was at the last cross-country meet, right around the four-mile mark. Everybody had passed me, just like the week before and the week before that. Everybody—except a girl from the other team. We were the only ones left in the last stretch of the course, the part that winds through the woods and comes out behind the school. Our shadows passed along

1

the ground slantwise; slowly they merged, then her shadow passed mine.

The soles of her sneakers swam up and down in front of me, first one, then the other, a grid of ridges that spelled out the upside-down name of the shoe company. My steps fell in time with hers. My feet went where her feet had just been. She leaned in around a corner, I leaned in around a corner. She breathed, I breathed.

Then she was gone.

I couldn't even picture her anymore. But what scared me, really scared me, was that I couldn't remember the moment when I'd stopped seeing her. And I knew then that if I couldn't see her, no one could see me.

Sounds from the track meet floated by. A whistle trilling. Muffled applause, the weak sputtering of gloved hands clapping. I was still running, but now I was off the path, heading away from the finish line, past the cars in the parking lot, the flagpole, and the HOME OF THE LIONS sign. Past fast-food places and car repair shops and video stores. Past the new houses and the park. Until, somehow, I was at the entrance to our development.

It was starting to get dark now, and I slowed down, walking past houses with windows of square yellow light where mothers were inside making dinner, past houses with windows of square blue light where kids were inside watching TV, to our house, where the driveway was empty and the lights were off.

I let myself in and flipped the light switch. There was an

explosion of light. The kitchen slid sideways, then righted itself.

I leaned against the door. "I'm home," I said to no one.

The room tilted left, then right, then straightened out. I grabbed hold of the edge of the dinner table and tried to remember if we stopped eating there because it was piled with junk or if it was piled with junk because we stopped eating there.

On the table there was a roll of batting, a glue gun, a doily, a 1997 Krafty Kitchens catalogue. Next to the catalogue was a special craft knife with the word EXACTO on the handle. It was sleek, like a fountain pen, with a thin triangular blade at the tip. I picked it up and laid the blade against the doily. The little knots came undone, just like that. I touched the blade to a piece of ribbon draped across the table and pressed, ever so slightly. The ribbon unfurled into two pieces and slipped to the floor without a sound. Then I placed the blade next to the skin on my palm.

A tingle arced across my scalp. The floor tipped up at me and my body spiraled away. Then I was on the ceiling looking down, waiting to see what would happen next. What happened next was that a perfect, straight line of blood bloomed from under the edge of the blade. The line grew into a long, fat bubble, a lush crimson bubble that got bigger and bigger. I watched from above, waiting to see how big it would get before it burst. When it did, I felt awesome. Satisfied, finally. Then exhausted.

• • •

I don't tell you any of this, though. I don't say anything. I just hug my elbows to my sides. My mind is a video on fast-forward. A video with no soundtrack.

And finally you sigh and stand up and say, "That's all we have time for today."

Twice a day we have Group. Group therapy, according to the brochure they give you at the admissions office, is the "keystone of the treatment philosophy" here at Sick Minds. The real name of the place is Sea Pines, even though there is no sea and there are no pines. My roommate, Sydney, who has a nickname for everything, calls it Sick Minds. Her nickname for me is S.T., for Silent Treatment.

We, by the way, are called guests. Our problems are called issues. Most of the girls are anorexic. They're called guests with food issues. Some are druggies. They're called guests with substance-abuse issues. The rest, like me, are assorted psychos. We're called guests with behavioral issues. The nurses are called attendants. And the place is called a residential treatment facility. It is not called a loony bin.

There aren't assigned seats in Group, but people tend to sit according to issues. The food-issue guests—Tara, a really skinny girl who has to wear a baseball cap to cover a bald spot where her hair fell out, and Becca, another really skinny girl who wears white little-girl tights that pool around her ankles and who came straight here from a hospital after she had a heart attack, and Debbie, a really, really overweight girl who says she's been here the longest—sit in a cluster of orange

4

plastic chairs next to Claire, the group leader. The substance-abuse guests—Sydney, who says she's addicted to every drug she's ever tried, and Tiffany, who seems normal but is here instead of going to jail for smoking crack—sit together on the other side of Claire's chair.

I sit by myself. I pick the chair the farthest from Claire and closest to the window, which they never open, even though it's always about a hundred degrees in here. Today, when Claire invites someone to start off, I decide to work on memorizing the order of the cars in the parking lot. *Brown, white, white, blue, beige. Brown, white, white, blue, beige.*

"All right, ladies," says Claire. "Who wants to go first?" Claire makes a little tent with her fingers and waits. I lean back in my usual spot in the circle, out of her line of vision.

Tara tugs on her hair, Debbie smoothes her sweatshirt over her stomach, and Becca slides off her chair and sits on the carpet at Debbie's feet, her legs tucked underneath her, Girl Scout style. No one answers.

Debbie cracks her weight-control gum. Tiffany, who for some reason wears a purse strapped across her chest at all times, fiddles with the latch.

"Ah, come on," Claire says. "Yesterday was visiting day. Surely somebody has something to say about that."

I add new cars to my list. *Brown, white, white, blue, beige, green, red. Brown, white, white, blue, beige, green, red.*

"OK, OK." Debbie says this like everyone was begging her to talk. "I might as well go first."

There's scattered squirming. Tiffany rolls her eyes. Tara,

5

who's so weak from not eating that she dozes off a lot during Group, leans her head against the wall; her eyes droop shut.

"It was terrible," Debbie says. "Not for me. But poor Becca." She gives Becca's thin shoulder a gentle squeeze. "Wait till I tell you what—"

Tiffany sighs and her enormous chest rises and falls. "Not for you, Debbie? Then how come I saw you at the nurses' desk last night begging for an escort to the vending machine?"

Debbie turns red.

"How come you're always so willing to talk about everyone else's problems?" Tiffany says. "What about yours? What happened at your visit, Debbie?"

Debbie regards her. "Nothing really."

"Really?" Sydney says, not unkindly.

"Really," says Debbie.

"That's crap," says Tiffany. Little drops of spit fly out of her mouth.

For Debbie this is a swear. She hates it when people swear. The temperature goes up to about 110 degrees.

"Debbie," Claire says gravely, "how do you feel about what Tiffany's saying?"

Debbie shrugs. "I don't care."

Sydney points a shaky finger in Debbie's direction. "You do so," she says. "You're pissed. Why don't you admit it, Debbie?"

Everyone waits.

"Well, I'd rather that she didn't swear." Debbie addresses this comment to Claire.

"Why don't you look at me?" Tiffany says. "Why don't you say, 'Tiffany, I don't like it when you say *crap*. Could you please watch your goddamn mouth?'"

Tara giggles. Sydney tries not to.

Debbie's mouth stretches into a tight smile, then her chin starts to quiver; I wipe my palms on my jeans.

"I know you all hate me because I'm not like the rest of you," she says. The effort of trying not to cry is making her face very red.

"I don't hate you," Becca says, craning her neck up toward Debbie.

"I don't know about the rest of you, but I want to graduate," Debbie says. "I don't want to just sit around here listening to people complain about their rotten childhoods."

Tiffany lifts her palms to the ceiling, charade for "I give up."

"Anyone else care to comment?" Claire says.

I hold very still. Claire's a hawk for body language. Biting your nails means you want to talk. Leaning forward means you want to talk. Leaning back means you want to talk. I don't move.

Sydney clears her throat. "I don't care if we talk about my visit," she says.

People exhale.

"My mom kept spritzing her mouth with Binaca but she'd

7

had a couple of pops before she got here. My dad kept checking his watch and making calls on his cell phone and my sister sat there doing her math homework."

The formula for converting Fahrenheit into Celsius enters my head uninvited. I try to calculate what 110 degrees Fahrenheit equals in Celsius.

"For my family . . ." Sydney taps the end of a pen, flicking an imaginary ash off the end of her imaginary cigarette. ". . . that's quality time."

People laugh, a little too hard.

"How did you feel when they were here?" Claire says.

"Fine." The smile on Sydney's face wilts slightly. "I mean, it's just like home."

This is a joke. No one laughs. Sydney surveys the group.

"Look. I have a strategy. Why expect anything? If you don't expect anything, you don't get disappointed."

Tara raises her hand. "Were you?"

Sydney doesn't understand. "Was I what?"

"Disappointed?"

Sydney still looks lost.

"I mean, I hope you don't take this the wrong way," Tara says. "But a minute ago you accused Debbie of pretending not to be pissed. Well, I think maybe you're pissed. At your mom and your dad and your sister." Tara sinks back in her chair; she gets tired just talking.

"I'm not mad at my sister," Sydney says. "It's not her fault. I mean, how would you like to spend your Saturday afternoon with a bunch of freaks?" She claps a hand over her

8

mouth. "No offense or anything. I mean, we spend all our time with freaks, but that's different. We are freaks."

A couple of people laugh.

Sydney goes on. "I don't care about my mom. I mean, what do you expect? That she'd wait till she got out of here for happy hour? Yeah, right. But my dad . . ."

I unfold and refold my arms across my chest. Bad move. Claire notices. Luckily, Sydney keeps talking.

"I don't know. He's not very good at stuff like this . . ." Sydney wrings the hem of her sweater; her hands are really shaking now. She laughs, sort of. Then, with no warning, she's crying. "I'm not pissed," she says. "It's . . . I'm just . . . I don't know, disappointed."

I squeeze my arms to my chest and feel embarrassed for Sydney, the way I used to in grade school when someone wet their pants. I hate Group. People always end up saying things that make them look pathetic.

"At least they came," says Tiffany. "My dad didn't even show."

Something else comes into my mind uninvited. It's an image of a dad walking up the sidewalk on visiting day, his hands stuffed in his jacket, his head tucked down against the wind. I tap on the window in the reception room. He glances up and I see that he has glasses and a red face and he's not my dad at all; he's someone else's dad. I go back to memorizing the cars in the parking lot.

"How do you feel about that?" Claire says to Tiffany.

"Screw him. That's how I feel."

9

I cross and recross my arms.

Claire pounces. "Callie."

At the sound of my name the heat closes in on me. I squint my eyes like I'm trying to make out something totally fascinating in the parking lot and think *Brown, white, white, blue, beige*. I lose my place and have to start again.

"Callie?" Claire's not giving up. "Do you want to tell us about your visit yesterday?"

There's a fly caught between the window and the screen. He seems sort of surprised each time he bangs into the glass. But he just staggers away, then rams into the glass again.

"Callie?"

I pull a curtain of hair down in front of my eyes and wait. After a while, someone from the other side of the circle starts talking. I can't really make out what she's saying, though. All I hear is the *zzzzzt-zzzzzt* of the fly banging into the window

There's a burst of chatter as everyone files out of Group. I hang behind the other girls, then go down the hall and check out the chalkboard next to the attendants' desk. On the board is a list of everyone's names and the treatments they go for after Group. Tiffany goes to Anger Management. Tara goes to Relaxation Therapy. Sydney and Tiffany also go to the infirmary for urine tests — to make sure they aren't taking anything. Becca, Tara, and Debbie go too — to make sure they *are* taking things: vitamins and food supplements for Tara and Becca, heart medicine for Becca, Prozac for Debbie. After that, Debbie goes to an exercise room where a trainer puts her on the treadmill. Tara and Becca get taken on a slow walk around the grounds to make sure they don't get on the treadmill.

There's nothing on the board next to my name. I don't get taken anywhere.

I duck around the corner before anyone can see me checking the board, because the other day I overheard Debbie, who spends a lot of time hanging around the attendants' desk, telling Becca that the people at Sick Minds were still trying to figure out what to do with me.

When you're a Level One (a new guest, or a guest exhibiting Inappropriate Behavior), you aren't allowed to go anywhere unsupervised. Level Twos (anybody who's accumulated ten points for Appropriate Behavior) are allowed to go to the day-room and to their appointments on their own, but they have to get escorts to go to the laundry room or the vending machine. Level Threes (people who are about to graduate, like Debbie) *are* the escorts. But even Level Threes with food issues have to get attendants or other Level Threes to escort them to the vending machines. It's complicated learning the Sick Minds system. It's easier being a Level One, if you ask me.

Since I'm a Level One, the only place I can go while everyone else is at treatment is Study Hall. It's supervised by an attendant named Cynthia, who sits in the front of the classroom answering multiple-choice questions in a big workbook. The only good thing about afternoon Study Hall, besides the fact that I'm usually the only one here, is that it's quiet. There are signs all over the place politely reminding us guests to respect each other's needs for silence; at least in here, I'm actually displaying Appropriate Behavior.

The walls are lined with cork board that other guests have covered with graffiti. I spend a lot of time reading their messages—names and comments like "This place sucks," or "Mrs. Bryant is a bitch." (Mrs. Bryant is either the lady who works in the admissions office or the head of the place, I'm not sure.) Mostly I listen to the rustling of paper as Cynthia turns the pages in her workbook.

I take my favorite seat in the back of the room, in the corner farthest away from Cynthia, and pretend to do the geometry assignment that my school faxed in. Really, I watch the dog who lives next to the maintenance shed. All he does is sleep and pace. Mostly he sleeps, but right now he's pacing back and forth in front of his doghouse. He's barking like mad at a delivery truck that's coming up the driveway. He trots to the end of his chain, barks, then turns and trots back. Then he turns around and does the same thing all over again. He's gone back and forth so many times, he's worn a dirt path in front of his house.

I sit there watching the dust fly as he paces back and forth, back and forth, while nobody pays attention to him. After a while I get up and move to a desk facing the wall.

Ruth, a Level Three from another group, arrives at the door, on time as always, to escort me to Individual. Ruth is this

12

very shy girl with bad skin and a way of ducking her chin inside her turtleneck; she just appears at the door every day at the same time, waiting for me to notice her. She looks so uncomfortable with her chin jammed into her chest and her hands shoved into her pockets that I always just get up and go with her.

The truth is, I don't mind being escorted by Ruth. I sort of like listening to our sneakers squeak along the hallway and not worrying that Ruth is going to try to make me talk. And I have a feeling that maybe Ruth doesn't mind escorting me either, because when we get to the waiting area outside your office, sometimes she hangs around a while, even though technically she doesn't have to.

After she goes, it's just me and the little white plastic UFO on the floor outside your office. Mrs. Bryant, who gave me my tour on the first day and who I've never seen since, said that the UFO—which looks like a plastic party hat with a motor inside—is called a white-noise machine. She said all the therapists have them outside their doors so people in the hall can't hear what the guests inside are saying. (The UFOs don't, however, drown out the yelling or the crying.)

Since I'm not talking (or yelling or crying), you could turn the UFO off during our session; that way, Sick Minds could save a little on the electric bill. I think about telling you that, but of course that would require talking, which would require turning on the UFO.

You open your door and invite me to come in. I consider lying down on the couch, thinking how nice it would be to

13

take a nap there for the next hour, but I sit in my usual spot, the corner farthest from you and your dead-cow chair. You sit down and ask about visiting day. "How was it for you?" you say.

I study your shoes. They're tiny black witch's shoes with silver buckles.

"What was it like seeing your family?"

Your shoes look like they're made of fabric, like they're too delicate to be worn in the real world.

"Is there anything you want to tell me?"

I consider saying something totally stupid. Something so boringly normal that you'll finally give up and leave me alone. I think about telling you that my mom wore her good wool coat, the one she wears to church and to doctor's appointments. Or about telling you that she looked tired, like the Before people in the Before and After pictures in her magazines. Or about how she started massaging her forehead as soon as she walked into the reception room.

Sam looked scared and excited all at once. He also seemed skinnier than ever; even though he was wearing a bulky red sweatshirt, his inhaler made a big bulge from inside his front shirt pocket. He let me hug him, then shoved a card at me. "I made this for you," he said. The card had pictures of cats all over it. Cats dancing. Cats jumping rope. Cats drinking tea. Cats playing basketball.

Sam's a really good artist for a third-grader, I imagine myself telling you, in a smart, sane voice. *But his spelling really sucks.* The card, which I hid under the mattress back in my room, says "Hop your feeling beter." It's signed by Sam and Linus.

Linus is our cat, I'd explain to you. You'd nod thoughtfully and I'd go on to explain that Linus has to live outside now, since the doctor said she was one of the things making Sam sick. I'd tell you that we named her Linus, even though she's a girl, because she used to carry around a sock in her mouth when she was a baby. *It looked like a security blanket, so we called her Linus*, I'd tell you. You'd smile. We'd make small talk. Except that I don't make talk, small or otherwise.

It was weird not saying anything to Sam when he handed me the card. I patted him on the head instead. Then my mom started sniffling, so I was able to walk away and get her a tissue from the coffee table. *That's one good thing about this place*, I'd tell you. *There are tissue boxes everywhere*.

I steered my mom and Sam over to a couch in the reception room. Sam looked around, his mouth hanging open like it does when he watches TV. "Why is this place called Sea Pines?"

He was waiting for me to answer, I think, but I was too busy pulling on a loose thread on the seat cushion. I pictured the whole couch coming unraveled and the three of us sitting on the floor in a giant pile of couch thread.

My mom was rubbing her temples. "It's just a name, Sam, like Pennbrook Manor, where Gram lived," she said finally.

"Where Gram died, you mean," Sam said.

"Well . . ." She gazed past Sam, around the reception room, trying to see what the other families were doing.

15

"That place smelled bad," Sam said.

"Well, Sam, this is different," my mom said. "This is a perfectly nice place."

"But what is it? Why is Cal here, anyhow?"

"Lower your voice," she said. "I already told you. She's not feeling well."

"She doesn't look sick."

"Shhh," she said. "Let's talk about something pleasant during the time we have, shall we?" She folded a tissue in her lap, then turned to me. "How's your roommate? Is she a nice girl?"

I got up and stood by the window, scanning the parking lot for my dad. I saw a man coming up the sidewalk and I tapped on the window; he lifted his head and I realized he wasn't my dad at all. The sliding doors opened and the man came in and gave Tara a big hug.

"If you're looking for Dad, he's not coming," Sam said.

My mom blew her nose.

I kept looking out the window; I didn't expect to see our car in the parking lot, since my mom doesn't drive anywhere anymore. She's terrified of big trucks and of missing her exit on the highway. She's also terrified of *E. coli* in hamburgers, childnappers at the mall, lead in the drinking water, and, of course, dust mites, animal fur, molds, spores, pollen, and anything else that might give Sam an asthma attack. I don't know what I expected to see in the parking lot. But I kept watching.

"Mommy," said Sam, "can I get some candy?" He was pointing to the vending machine.

My mom said yes and I thought about how Sam could just walk over and buy himself a Snickers, without an escort. My mom gave him a bunch of quarters, and he skipped, actually skipped, over to the vending machine.

"Daddy's putting in some extra hours," my mom whispered when Sam was out of earshot. "He's trying to make a little extra money."

She folded her tissue into a neat square, then a smaller one, then an even smaller one. Keeping track made me dizzy.

"We got a letter from the insurance company." She was speaking so quietly, I had to lean in to hear her. "They won't pay for your . . . your treatment here."

The reception room lifted off the foundation, floated for a second, then became solid again. I checked to see if my mom noticed.

"They say they won't pay because this thing you do, you know, cutting yourself, they say it's self-inflicted. They don't cover things that are self-inflicted."

The room hovered in the air again, then the floor slid away and I was on the ceiling looking down at a play. The character who was the mom was still talking; the one who was me was fiddling with a piece of thread from the couch. Offstage, a Snickers bar clattered down the insides of a vending machine. I tried to concentrate on what the mother was saying. Something about seeing friends at the mall. "I told them you were under the weather," she said. The tissue, now a tiny, tiny square, wobbled in and out of focus. "Are you keeping up with your schoolwork?"

The mother's mouth was moving, but the character who was me was walking away, through the maze of sofas and coffee tables and more sofas until finally I was in the visitors' restroom, rubbing my wrist along the teeth of the paper towel dispenser. It was like my whole body was just this one spot on my arm that was begging to be scratched, carved, cut—anything, anything—for relief. There was a jab, bright beads of blood, and finally I was OK. I pulled my shirtsleeve down, pressed my cheek against the cool tile wall for a minute, then walked back into the reception room like everything was fine.

Except that the reception room was practically empty. I'd been in the restroom only a minute, I thought, but my mom and Sam and just about everybody else were gone. I made my way through the grid of sofas and coffee tables, forcing myself to concentrate, to slow down, so I didn't break into a run.

I finally found Sam down the hall, sitting by himself in the game room, this dark little library-type place where they keep board games and cards that nobody ever plays. The game room is my favorite place here; I go there just about every night during free time to get away from the fake laughter from the TV in the dayroom, and the fake applause from the TV at the attendants' desk, and all the radios and the

18

blow dryers in the dorm. When I came in, Sam turned around and grinned, showing off his big, new rabbity front teeth.

"Cal! Look what game they have," he said. "Connect Four."

Connect Four, a kind of tic-tac-toe where you have to get four checkers in a row in a plastic stand, is our favorite game to play together. We started playing it when Sam first got sick and he wasn't allowed to run around anymore. In the beginning I let him win, because he was younger and because he was sick. Now he beats me every time.

I don't know how he does it, but Sam has this way of seeing two or three ways to win. Meanwhile, I use up all my moves trying to block him—or trying to get four in a row in a straight, up-and-down line—until Sam yells "Gotcha," and points to some diagonal row I completely overlooked.

"Wanna play?" he said.

I checked to make sure no one was around. *Sure*, I wanted to say. *Sure.* I willed myself to speak, but nothing happened. I sent commands from my brain to my mouth. Nothing. I wondered if a person's voice muscles can forget how to work if they're not used for a long time.

I stared out the window for a while, like the answer might be out there. I nodded.

Sam took the black checkers, I took the red. That's the way it always is. We don't even have to discuss it. The only sound, as we sat at the card table playing, was the click of checkers dropping into their slots. I imagined myself saying chatty, big-sister things—about Linus, about Sam's hockey card collection—but just thinking about talking was exhausting.

Sam plunked a checker into the plastic stand; he pointed to a row of four blacks that seemed to appear out of nowhere.

"Gotcha," he said. "Wanna play again?" He didn't wait. "OK," he answered himself.

It dawned on me then that Sam understood. Somehow, he knew—in his weird, wise, eight-year-old way—that I wasn't talking. So he talked for both of us. I answered by putting a red checker in the center slot. It was my favorite opening move.

"Cal," he said, shaking his head, an old, tired Sam who pretended to be disappointed in me. "You need to think laterally."

I watched while he put a black checker in the last row.

"That means seeing things a couple of different ways," he said. "Mr. Weiss says I'm good at that."

I put another red checker above the first one and wondered who Mr. Weiss was.

"He's my tutor." Another black checker went in, blocking my row. "He comes to the house."

That meant Sam was too sick to go to school again. Which meant my mom must be more upset than ever. Which meant my dad would be spending more time than ever at work—or more time out with customers, or people he hoped would be customers but somehow never turned into customers.

"Don't worry," said Sam. "We don't have to pay for it. School pays for it."

I had no idea where to put another checker, so I tried to start another row from the bottom.

"Gotcha!" Sam pointed to a diagonal row of black checkers. "Lateral thinking, Cal."

He set up the game so we could play again.

"Mom went to talk to one of your, you know, your teachers." Something about the way he said that, something about how it was such a little-kid thing to say, made me feel bad.

He put a black checker in the last row. "She went to find her when you were in the bathroom."

I put a red checker in the center slot again. I didn't have the energy for lateral thinking.

Sam held his checker in the air, poised to move. "When are you coming home, Cal? No one will tell me anything."

We sat there a while, I couldn't tell how long. Sam's face went from hopeful, to serious, to worried, to something I couldn't quite read.

"It's OK," he said finally. "It's just that Linus misses you."

I look up and take in the sight of you, still sitting there, your ankles crossed, your notebook in your lap. I hate that notebook because I know some random thing—like your chair reminding me of a dead cow—could end up in there, proof that I'm crazy. But what I really hate is how every day when I come in, you turn to a fresh page and write in the date, and how every day when I leave and you walk me to the door, I can see that the whole page is empty.

You cap your pen and stand up. It must be time to go.

The cafeteria here has a humid, steamed-vegetable smell that's enough to give anyone food issues. What's worse than the smell, though, is the noise. Sometimes, like when I'm in Study Hall or the game room, I can pretend that this place is a boarding school, but when all the guests from all the other groups are together in the cafeteria shouting and laughing and arguing and eating, you know you're in a loony bin.

Our group has to sit together at meals. Sydney sets her tray down in the empty space next to me.

"I've figured out the Sick Minds food philosophy." She says this to the table at large.

The food-issue people lean in attentively. I twirl my pasta around and around my fork until it slips off.

"There are four basic food groups here: pasta, purees, puddings, and potatoes," she says. "They only serve things that begin with a *p*."

Debbie sighs.

"Seriously," Sydney says, "have you ever noticed?"

"I'm sick of pasta," Tara says. "All those carbohydrates are an issue for me."

"Yeah," says Tiffany. "This stuff is crap."

"We had chicken last week," says Debbie.

"Yes, Debbie, we remember," says Tiffany. "It was the high point of your life."

22

Because we guests can't be trusted with real silverware, the food usually has to be mushy enough to eat with plastic spoons. Last Thursday, though, we had chicken à la king, and since Debbie's the only Level Three in our group she got to hand out stubby plastic forks and knives. She also got to collect them at the end of the meal. "It's sort of like being on a picnic," she said.

Sydney changes the subject. "Look," she says, pointing across the room. "It's the Ghost."

A woman with a gray braid down to her waist is waltzing around the salad bar. She's wearing a long white dress and her arms are stretched out like she's got an imaginary partner.

"She's from Humdinger," says Sydney.

"What's that?" asks Tara.

"The wing where they keep the real psychos."

"You mean Hammacher," Debbie says.

"Humdinger," says Sydney. "You have to be a real humdinger to get in."

People laugh.

"Once you get in, you never get out."

No one laughs this time.

Dinner doesn't take long. That's because the first person back to the dayroom gets the remote control. Tonight, though, there seems to be a delay; I pick up from the chatter that something special is going on.

"That's great," Debbie coos to Becca. "You're doing really great."

Becca lowers her lashes and picks a crumb off the corner of her brownie. Then she puts the crumb on her plate and cuts it in half with her plastic spoon.

"You're going to eat the whole brownie, right?" Debbie says this loudly, for everyone's benefit.

Becca nods demurely. "C'mon," she says, giving Debbie's arm a nudge with her thin little elbow. "You know I can't eat if you're all watching."

"OK, OK," Debbie announces. "No one look at Becca."

Sydney pinches her thumb and index finger together, giving Becca the A-OK sign. Then everyone makes a big show of looking away. I push my chair back, finger the metal strip around the edge of the table, and stare underneath at people's feet. The din of plates and cups clattering and people shouting ebbs, then picks up, louder than ever. That's when I see Becca slide the brownie off her plate into her lap. She wads it up in her napkin, mashes it flat, and stuffs it in her pocket.

After a while Becca says it's OK for people to look again. There are oohs and ahhs. Three chimes sound, signaling the end of dinner; Debbie says we should let Becca be in charge of the remote control that night.

Later, while the other girls are in the dayroom watching *Jeopardy*, I hide in a nook near the attendants' desk, holding a pile of laundry and waiting until the coast is clear. I have to do laundry every couple of days because just about all my mom packed for me is pajamas. Nightgowns, actually. Brand-new ones with daisies and bows.

I watch for Rochelle, the bathroom attendant, to leave the desk and take her post on the orange plastic chair between the toilets and the showers. Then I inch up to the desk and wait for Ruby to notice me.

Ruby's skin is indigo and her hair is the silver of an antique teapot. But the thing about Ruby is her shoes: they're old-fashioned white nurse's shoes. Unlike the other attendants, who dress like they're going to an office or to the mall or something, Ruby wears thick white stockings and real nurse's shoes. The first night I got here, the only way I was able to fall asleep was listening for the squeak of her footsteps on the slick green linoleum as she made her rounds. I can't say why exactly, but I trust those shoes.

Ruby's sitting down, knitting, something pink, maybe a baby blanket. As I watch her knobby hands fly over the yarn in time with the whish and click of the knitting needles, I wonder what Ruby does when she's not at Sick Minds. If she's somebody's grandmother, maybe, or somebody's next-door neighbor.

She smiles when she sees me. "Need an escort to the laundry room?" she says.

I keep my gaze locked on the pink thing unfurling beneath her knitting needles.

"Yes, indeed," she answers herself. "Give me a sec. OK?" She doesn't wait for me to respond. "OK," she says.

Like Sam, Ruby doesn't expect me to say anything. She's happy to do the talking for both of us. I lean against the desk and watch while she sweeps the yarn around her finger and finishes off a few more stitches. Then she puts her knitting on the desk and hoists her short, dense body out of her chair. Her keys jingle and she says, "OK, baby. Let's go."

I try to figure out the right amount of space to keep between us as we walk down the hall. At first I stay close to the wall. But that feels wrong, so I move closer and try to match my stride to Ruby's; I bump into her, then veer away. After that, I stay next to the wall. When we get to the stairs, Ruby holds the door open, then lets it fall shut behind us. We're in our own small world now, the hushed world of the stairway, where all the noise from the dorm—the constant music and talking and TV voices—doesn't exist.

She stops a second and holds out her hand. In it is a small butterscotch candy, the kind my Gram used to keep in a dish in her living room.

"Go on, take it," she says. "It's all right. You're not one of those food-disorder girls, right?" She tucks the candy into my hand. "Right."

"Besides, a little something sweet never hurt anybody," Ruby says. "I may not have a degree in psychology, but I know some home truths." She taps the space between her breasts, as if that's where home truths might be stored.

When we get down to the laundry room, Ruby unlocks the cupboard where the detergent is kept; then she leans against the wall and watches as I put my jeans and shirts in

26

the wash, measuring and remeasuring the soap powder, arranging and rearranging the clothes, and hoping Ruby will say more about her home truths.

But she doesn't. All I hear is the sound of plastic crinkling as she unwraps a butterscotch candy for herself. "All right, baby," Ruby says when I close the lid of the washing machine. "Let's get ourselves back upstairs."

On the way back up, we pass a fire exit sign with a diagram and a big red arrow next to the words YOU ARE HERE.

And I wonder, if Sick Minds was on fire or something, would I be able to scream?

There's a lot of crying here at night. Since there are no doors on any of the rooms, the crying—or moaning, or sobbing—floats out into the hallway. Sometimes I lie in bed imagining a river of sobs flowing by, leaving little puddles of misery on each threshold.

When I first got here, I spent a lot of time trying to identify the crier by voice and location. Someone nearby mews like a kitten. That, I think, is Tara. Someone down the hall has a choppy cry that starts out sounding like laughing. That, I'm pretty sure, is Debbie. But after a while I decided that trying to guess which crying went with which girl just made it harder to fall asleep.

So I came up with a game that helps take my mind off the crying.

It's simple. I lie there and focus all my attention on the sound of Sydney's breathing. Sydney, who falls asleep right

27

after lights out, sleeps on her back, her mouth wide open. If I listen hard enough, I can hear her breath go in with a slight *ahh* sound, and out with a *hah* sound. And if I try really hard, I can tell the exact moment when the inhale turns into an exhale.

Today, when Ruth walks me to your office, she hangs around longer than usual, kicking the toe of one sneaker with the other. I kick the toe of one sneaker with the other, notice that we're doing the same thing, and stop. Ruth stops too, then takes her hands out of her pockets one at a time and clasps them in front of her. Slowly she lifts her chin, until finally, after a lot of effort, she's looking at me straight on. Then she smiles.

A smile seems out of place on Ruth's blotchy red face, like it's something she doesn't do very often, like it's something she's practicing.

And I try to let her see, by not looking away, that I don't mind if she practices on me.

Then she's gone and I'm listening to her shoes squeak back to the ward.

You lean forward in your dead-cow chair; I pull back.

"I have a theory," you say.

I decide then that I want to know exactly how many stripes there are on your wallpaper. *Tan, white. Tan, white, tan, white.*

"It's just a hunch," you say.

28

Tan. White. Tan. White.

"I don't know why you're not speaking to anyone . . ."

The stripes turn faint and it's hard to see where the tan stops and the white starts.

"But I would guess that not talking takes an enormous effort."

I picture myself running after school, something that takes a lot of effort, at least at first. After about the first mile, though, the white-out effect would kick in. I'd stop noticing the trees, or the road, or whether it was cold, or even where I was going. It was like someone came along with a giant bottle of white-out, erasing everything around me. Sometimes I'd even forget I was running and all of a sudden I'd see a building or a road I'd never seen before and I'd realize I'd gone too far. The white-out effect had stopped. I'd turn around and run home then, wondering if I'd have the energy to make it.

"It must take a lot of energy," you say.

I blink.

"Not talking. It must be very tiring."

I watch granules of dust slowly drift through a shaft of afternoon sun, and all at once I *am* tired. Something inside me sags, like a seam giving way. But my brain fights back.

My mom's the one who gets tired. My mom and Sam. My mom gets tired washing everything with antibacterial spray and making special food for Sam and scrubbing the lint out of all the filters and air-vent covers to keep Sam from having an asthma attack, so tired that sometimes she has to rest all

29

day. And Sam sometimes gets so tired just getting ready for school that he has to go straight back to bed.

Which means staying absolutely quiet when I get home from school so they can rest. Which could be for ten minutes or ten hours. Which means it's up to me to do the spraying and cleaning. Which still doesn't stop Sam from having an attack. Which means he could be in the hospital for a couple of hours or a couple of days. Which means my mom will stay there around the clock, until she gets so tired she has to come home and rest. Which means it's up to me to do more spraying and cleaning. Which means I just don't get tired.

". . . you're in a situation here where a lot of things are beyond your control."

I look up and it occurs to me that you've been talking all along.

"Just about everything you do here is determined by forces outside your control—what time you get up, how often you go to Group, how often you come to see me. Am I right?"

I understand now that you're talking about Sick Minds; I go back to counting the stripes on the wallpaper.

"Sometimes when we're in situations where we feel we're not in control, we do things, especially things that take a lot of energy, as a way of making ourselves feel we have some power."

The tan and white stripes melt together.

"But Callie." Your voice is so quiet, I have to stop counting a minute to hear it. "You'd have so much more power . . . if you would speak."

Usually I try to be the last one to use the bathroom in the morning. That way, I don't have to see the other girls looking all soft and sad the way people do after they've been dreaming. This morning, though, when I walk past Rochelle, the bathroom attendant, I see Tara standing at a sink in her nightgown and baseball cap, putting on makeup. I pick the sink farthest away and make a big deal out of putting toothpaste on my brush.

After a while I stand back at just the right angle so I can see, down the row of mirrors, a dozen reflections of Tara. Tara taking off her baseball cap. Tara touching a comb gingerly to her head. Tara arranging thin, colorless strands of hair around a bald spot. Something about that bare patch of scalp makes me feel so bad I have to turn away.

"Think we'll make it in time for breakfast?"

I study the column of water streaming out of the faucet. From the corner of my eye, I see that Tara has put her baseball cap back on; she's talking to me.

"We better hurry," she says. "Debbie says we're having pancakes." Tara's voice is surprisingly deep and womanly, considering she weighs only 92 pounds. Last week in Group she announced that this was a new high for her. A couple of people clapped. She cried.

I turn up the water full blast and stare at it like something

31

about it is very, very important. I can't see Tara, but I can feel her standing a few sinks away watching me and suddenly I feel bad giving the silent treatment to someone who weighs only 92 pounds and has to wear a baseball cap to cover up a bald spot.

The rushing water gets louder, then softer, then louder. Tara moves toward the door where Rochelle is sitting on the orange plastic chair, reading *People* magazine.

"Do you really want us to ignore you?" There's nothing mean about the way Tara says this; there's nothing in her voice except curiosity.

I waste as much time as I can brushing my teeth. Eventually, she's gone.

Today is linen-exchange day. All of us guests have to line up in the laundry room and hand in our old sheets and towels and get new ones. Everyone displays Appropriate Behavior during linen exchange, probably because Doreen, the custodial worker in charge, takes it very seriously. Each week she hangs hand-lettered signs all over the laundry room, signs with lots of capital letters and exclamation points. "Line forms to the right of the Attendant!" says one. "Please have your linens ready for Presentation to the Attendant!" says another.

I'm standing in line—to the right of the Attendant, with my linens ready for Presentation—when Sydney and Tara come up behind me. I can tell from the cigarette smell that they've just come in from the smoking porch, where everyone else hangs out between sessions.

"Hi, S.T."

Heat creeps up my cheeks. I feel bad not talking to Sydney, since she always says hello to me like I'm a normal person. I hold myself rigid and wait.

"These signs crack me up," Sydney says after a while. I relax a little, once I figure out she's talking to Tara. "This one's my favorite."

I can't help but listen in.

"'Guests are kindly requested to refrain from removing their mattress pads at the end of their stay.'" Sydney reads Doreen's sign in a deep, official-sounding voice. "Like someone's going to say, 'Hmmm. What souvenir can I bring home from my stay at Sick Minds? Oh, I know! A mattress pad!'"

I picture Doreen, suddenly, in a tug-of-war with someone over a mattress pad. I can see Doreen pulling the emergency alarm, then rolling around on the floor trying to wrestle one of her beloved mattress pads away from a guest. A giggle creeps up my throat. I swallow. A full-fledged brawl is raging in my mind's eye, with guests and attendants slugging it out over mattress pads. I bite the insides of my cheeks. I dig my nails into my palms. It's no good. I bolt out of line and run for the steps.

"Where are you going?" Doreen yells. "That's a violation, you hear?"

The door swings shut behind me and I'm in the cool,

muffled world of the hallway. I take the steps two at a time, stomping so hard that the echo drowns out the strange, stifled sound of me trying not to laugh.

The attendant in the game room that night is one I've never seen before, young, smiley and obviously new. She says hi and asks if I want to play Scrabble. "How 'bout Trivial Pursuit?" she says. "I'm really good at that."

I get out the Connect Four box and sit down with my back to her. Then I start playing against myself. I imitate Sam's lateral thinking strategy, making moves all over the place, instead of starting with the same opening move and the same boring way of trying to build an obvious straight line. After a while the smiley young attendant gets up and leaves to talk to another attendant at the desk, keeping an eye on me through the window.

Soon the Connect Four grid is a hopeless mess of red and black checkers; there are blocked rows everywhere and no way to make a straight line. I'm staring at the game when a shadow comes over the table.

You're standing next to me suddenly, in a long blue coat and scarf, holding a purse and keys. I sit up—and wait for you to tell me, in your real-life clothes, with your car keys and your house keys, that you're leaving, that you're quitting, that you're giving up on me.

But you don't say anything. The room gets warmer and warmer and the minutes stretch out and fold back on themselves the way they do in your office and you just stand there, tapping your upper lip with your index finger and studying the game. I decide to pretend I don't care that you're there.

I pick up a red checker, hold it a minute, poised to drop it into the center slot, then pull back, seeing right away that this would be a dumb move. I move the checker, hold it above another slot, study this possibility, and see that it would be a mistake too. Finally I put the checker on the table, lean back, and hide inside my hair.

You shift your weight from one foot to the other and I catch a hint of fragrance. It's a cool, familiar smell, sort of like the lavender sachets my Gram used to make.

You pick up the red checker and drop it into a slot on the end. All at once a diagonal row of four checkers appears— surprising and obvious at the same time.

"There you go," you say. "I think that's the move you were looking for."

You rest your hand on my shoulder for just a second, and I feel sleepy suddenly, the way I did in your office this afternoon. Then you're gone. I don't play another round. I just sit in the game room until the last trace of lavender evaporates.

The next day, after everyone else comes in from the smoking porch and we take our regular seats in Group, Claire announces that a new girl is joining us. She asks if someone will get an extra chair. "Put it there, please," she tells Sydney. "Next to Callie."

I sit very, very still.

The door squeaks open and the new girl comes in. She's

tiny, with dyed black hair held back in kiddie barrettes, red lipsticked lips, and the palest, whitest skin I've ever seen. She's wearing ripped jeans and a sweatshirt.

Claire gestures toward the empty spot next to me and invites her to sit down. The girl slides into the chair, then grabs the seat, scraping the legs back and forth on her little patch of floor, trying to get settled. Her chair bangs into mine. The impact reverberates all through me.

"Oops," she says.

Claire asks if anyone is willing to make the introductions, but it seems like everyone has suddenly gotten shy. So Claire goes around the circle giving names but not issues.

The new girl says her name so quickly I can't tell if it's Amanda or Manda. Then, when no one says anything, she says, "Jesus Christ, it's hot in here."

Claire asks Amanda/Manda if she wants to tell us why she's at Sick Minds. Amanda/Manda pulls off her sweatshirt; I feel every movement through my chair.

There's a gasp from across the circle. Debbie's hand is clapped over her mouth and the other girls are staring at the new girl.

Her sweatshirt is on the floor and she's sitting there in a little white undershirt holding her arms out so everyone can see a geometry of scars crisscrossing her inner arms: scars in parallel lines running up to her elbow, bisecting lines, obtuse angles. Scratched into the skin above her wrists are words. In pink scar tissue on one arm it says "Life." On the other it says "Sucks."

I pull my sleeves down around my thumbs and pinch the fabric tight.

"I don't really need to be here," she says. "Some do-good English teacher thought I was trying to kill myself."

There's scattered fidgeting, then silence. "You're not?" Sydney finally says.

"As *if*," Amanda/Manda says.

"Then why do you do it?"

"Beats me," she says. Then, right away, "Low self-esteem. Poor impulse control. Repressed hostility. Right?" She addresses all this to Claire.

Claire doesn't answer, so Amanda/Manda turns back to Sydney. "Listen, I don't see how what I do is so different from people who get their tongues pierced. Or their lips. Or their ears, for Chrissakes. It's my body."

She glances around the circle; no one budges.

"It's body decoration. Like tattoos." She keeps talking, like she's been in the middle of a conversation that everybody else happened to walk in on. Like we're new, not her. "It's better than people who bite their nails till they bleed. I mean, they're actually eating their own flesh. They're like cannibals."

Tiffany, who bites her nails until they bleed, tucks her hands under her thighs.

"I mean, why is everyone so upset? It's freedom of expression, right?"

I grind the hem of my sleeve between my fingers. The frantic barking of a dog rings in the distance. Amanda/

- 37

Manda is saying something about an article she read in a magazine. I turn my head ever so slightly to catch the words.

"You know, they used to bleed people all the time back in the old days," she says. "When they were sick. It's an endorphin rush."

"And . . ." All heads swivel in the direction of Claire's voice. "Does it make you feel better?" Claire says.

"Absolutely." Amanda/Manda shifts in her chair. "It's a high. I mean, you feel amazing. No matter how bad you felt before. It's a rush. Like suddenly you're alive."

"And you want to do it again, don't you?" Claire says.

My fingers are numb from pinching my shirtsleeve.

"Yeah. So?"

"Let me rephrase that," Claire says slowly. "You *need* to do it again."

The new girl leans forward in her chair, her dark eyes blazing. "Not me," she says. "I can control it. I always control it." She folds her arms across her chest; her elbow nudges mine. I jump.

"What about you, Callie?" Claire's voice is loud. "Can *you* control it?"

The room is dead quiet. Debbie stops cracking her weight-control gum. Even the dog stops barking. Far off, down the hall, a phone trills, once, twice, three times. It's answered by an invisible voice.

"Callie?"

I feel the new girl turn to regard me.

I nod.

And I can feel the rest of the group exhale.

I spend the rest of the session counting the stitches on my sneaker and hating this Amanda/Manda person, hating Claire, hating this whole stupid place. Because now everybody knows why I'm here.

I'm at my usual place at dinner that night, at the far end of the long rectangular table, trying to make each mouthful last for twenty chews. That way, it takes me just as long to eat as it does for everybody else to eat and talk. The other girls are turned away, discussing some kind of petition. Sydney says she wants pizza. Tara suggests lowfat yogurt. The petition, I deduce, must be about the food. Becca says she wants croutons without gluten, whatever that is.

"How about an ice cream bar?" Debbie says. "Like a salad bar. You can go back as many times as you want."

"Yeah, right," says Tiffany. "That's just what you need."

"I was *kidding*," Debbie says.

"What do *you* want?" It's a voice I don't recognize right away, the new girl's.

When I look up, two rows of heads are turned in my direction. This reminds me, suddenly, of a book my Gram gave me when I was little, about Madeline, the little French girl who lived with twelve little girls in two straight lines.

I pick up my plastic spoon and sculpt my mashed potatoes into a little hill.

"We don't know about her," I hear Debbie say. "She doesn't talk."

I make a little mashed potato ski slope, then flatten it with my spoon. The other girls go back to talking about the petition and I decide that dinner's over for me, that it's time to bring my tray up to the conveyor belt that takes all the dirty dishes and cups and leftover food through a window into the dish room, where they disappear.

I stand and try to squeeze between the chairs at our table and the ones behind us. The space is tight and I hold my tray high so I don't bump into anybody. I pass safely behind Sydney, then Tara. When I get to the new girl, she rocks back; my toe stubs the leg of her chair. Milk sloshes out of my glass and down the back of her sweatshirt.

"Jesus!" She practically spits out the word. "Why don't you watch what you're doing?" She's wiping her sweatshirt with a paper napkin. They all look at me, six sick girls in two straight lines, waiting for me to do something.

Somehow I navigate through the sea of tables and chairs and more chairs until I'm finally at the conveyor belt.

The lunchroom attendant, a heavy woman who sits guard over the trash cans to keep track of how much food the anorexics throw out, gives me a bothered expression, then goes back to her paperback.

Across the room, a dish explodes on the floor; there's the obligatory smattering of applause. The attendant gets up, turns her book facedown on her chair, and brings a broom and dustpan over to the girl who dropped her dish.

I stand in front of the blue trash can marked "Recyclables" and finger the edge of my aluminum pie plate,

40

aware that no one's watching me, that all I'd have to do is rip the pie plate in half to get a nice sharp cutting edge. The clatter of dishes and conversation dims to a hush as I slip the thin, impossibly light disk of aluminum into my pocket. I'm calm, finally, because I know that even if I don't use it right away, I have what I need.

That night, Sydney tosses and turns and fusses with her blankets for almost an hour after lights-out. I lie on my back and count the seconds, praying for her to fall asleep, so I can hear the sound of her steady in-out breathing—so *I* can fall asleep.

She rolls over, facing my direction.

"Callie?" she whispers. The space between our twin beds is only a foot or two.

I hold my breath and try to pretend I'm asleep.

"Callie? Callie," she says. "Do you still do it?"

I hold very still.

"I mean, are you still, you know, cutting yourself?"

From down the hall comes the faint squeaking of Ruby's nurse's shoes as she makes her rounds. From the sound of it, Ruby's still four doors away. I think of it as a problem on a standardized test: if Ruby's shoes squeak every 2.5 seconds and she's four rooms away, how long till she reaches our door?

"Lookit, Callie." Sydney blows out a gust of air, the way she does when she's smoking an imaginary cigarette in Group. "It's OK with me if you don't want to talk."

41

Just a few squeaks until Ruby's at our door. People who aren't asleep when Ruby comes around have to take sleeping pills. Everyone is afraid of those pills—even the substance-abuse guests.

Sydney sighs. "Just don't, you know . . . please don't hurt yourself."

Tears, warm and sudden, sting the corners of my eyes, but I don't cry. Sam cries. My mom cries. I don't cry. I roll over as Ruby passes by. She pauses outside our door a minute, a brief interruption in the steady *squeak*, *squeak* of her shoes. Then she moves on. And after a while I figure Sydney must have fallen asleep, because finally I can hear the steady in-out of her breathing.

On the way to your office the next day, Ruth clears her throat. She puts her hand over her mouth, then says she has something to tell me, that this is the last day she'll be my escort. Her voice is small, unsteady. "I'm graduating," she says. "Tomorrow."

She smiles a practice smile, and one of my dad's favorite dumb jokes comes to mind. The joke is about a family riding along in a brand-new convertible. The car hits a bump, and one of the kids, a girl named Ruth, falls out. But the family keeps on driving. *Ruth*lessly. "Get it?" he would say, grinning. "Ruthlessly?"

Sick Minds will be a Ruthless place once she's gone. I would like to tell Ruth this, give this joke to her as a graduation gift. But then she is gone and I'm sitting next to the

UFO—Ruthlessly—and wondering how she got better without looking any different.

You furrow your brow and ask me to please look at you a minute. I look past you, out the window, at a squirrel sitting on the end of a branch.

"Callie," you say softly. "I want you to think about whether you want to continue coming to see me."

The squirrel nibbles on his acorn, looks around suspiciously, then goes back to his lunch.

"This—the two of us sitting here every day, with me watching you count the stripes on the wallpaper—isn't helping you."

The squirrel freezes; the branch quivers as another squirrel scrambles toward him.

"And Callie . . . I believe you want help."

The squirrels are gone, but the branch is still quivering. I steal a glimpse at you; you're pretty, I realize, and youngish. You wrap your hands around your knees, like we're two girlfriends, just hanging out, talking. I go back to counting the stripes on the wallpaper.

After a while, I hear your dead-cow chair groan. You sigh. "OK," you say. "That's all for today."

The clock says we still have fifty minutes left. But you've already capped your pen and closed your notebook.

I keep my hand on your doorknob a minute, standing in the waiting area outside your office, wondering what I'm supposed to do now. There's no one to escort me and there's no place to escort me to.

I picture you on the other side of the door, closing the manila file with my name on it, all the empty sheets of notebook paper, from all the days I came and sat in your office counting the stripes on the wallpaper, spilling into the trash. And it occurs to me that I'm alone—really alone—for the first time since I got here.

I let go of the knob and move away from your door, slowly, then faster, down the hall, not really knowing where I'm going, just going. I pass a supply closet, then a door with a large red bar and a metal flag on it marked "For Emergency Use Only," and I wonder if an alarm really would ring if I opened it, if it would be like a prison escape movie, if Rochelle would throw down her magazine and come running, if Doreen would drop her linens and man the searchlight, if the other girls would stumble out of their rooms and ask what was going on. But my feet carry me past the Emergency Use Only door, back the way I came with Ruth a few minutes ago, back to Study Hall.

The door is closed, though. There's no sign or anything. Of course it's closed; Study Hall is over. Everyone is at Individual or Anger Management or Art Therapy. Everyone except me.

Down the hall I hear keys jingle. Marie, the daytime bathroom attendant, is taking up her post on the orange chair. I walk in her direction, trying to act normal.

She barely notices as I go past; she doesn't ask me what

I'm doing here without an escort or why I'm here when I'm supposed to be somewhere else.

I pick a stall down at the end and stand inside facing the toilet. I put my hand on the handle and imagine myself imitating the man on the radio, the man who says, "Testing. Testing. One. Two. Three." The handle is cold and wet with condensation; I wipe my hand on my jeans and pray that the sound of the toilet flushing will be loud enough. "This is a test," the man says. "This is *only* a test."

I clear my throat and jiggle the handle.

"Everything OK in there?" Marie calls out.

I grip the handle.

"I said, is everything OK in there?"

I can hear the scrape of Marie's chair on the tile floor as she stands up.

I push on the handle. A great roar comes up from the toilet bowl. I lean over like I'm going to be sick, but nothing comes out.

Forty-five minutes is a long time. You can divide it into nine five-minute segments, five nine-minute segments, three fifteen-minute segments, fifteen three-minute segments, or two twenty-two-and-a-half-minute segments. That's if you have a watch. If you have to spend it hiding in the laundry room listening for the sounds of footsteps overhead telling you that people are finished with Art Therapy or Anger Management or Individual, you have to time it just right so you come upstairs not too early, not too late, so that you can slip into Group right on schedule without anyone even noticing that you were gone.

As I'm leaving Study Hall for dinner, Tara's coming toward me carrying a bouquet of tulips. The flowers, which are gigantic in her thin, little-girl arms, are dripping, even though she's cupped her hand under the stems.

I consider turning back, pretending I left something in Study Hall, but Tara calls out to me. "Can you believe it?" she says. "They took the vase away at the front desk. Glass."

Here at Sick Minds we guests are not allowed to have any "sharps"— glass or thumbtacks or CDs or ballpoint pens or razors. Sydney keeps making a joke about how there's only one difference between the employees here and the guests; the guests, she says, are the ones with hairy legs.

Tara stops a few feet in front of me. My feet drag to a stop, too. "Here," she says. She disentangles one flower from the bunch and holds it out toward me, the way Sam did when he gave me the "Hop your feeling beter" card. Then, before I can take it or not take it, she places the flower on top of my geometry book.

She breezes past, humming. It takes an enormous effort for me to start walking again.

Sydney and I are sitting on our beds after dinner studying when the new girl knocks on our doorless door frame. She's wearing a tank top, cutoffs, and flip-flops; I feel cold just

46

looking at her. "It's for you," she says, cocking her chin in my direction.

I don't understand. Is her outfit for me? To make me look at her? To make me feel cold?

"The phone," she says. "It's for you." She turns to go, then pauses. "Hey, how do you give someone the silent treatment over the phone? I mean, how do they know if you're even there?"

My cheeks flame. I put down my geometry book, get up from my bed, and follow her down the hall, counting the number of times her yellow flip-flops thwack against the glossy green linoleum.

She pauses a moment before turning in to her room, which is right next to the phone booth. "Don't worry," she says. "I won't listen to you not talking."

I sit down on the little curved seat in the phone booth and reach up to close the door. But there is no door. I forget sometimes that there are no doors here. I pick up the receiver, still warm from the grip of the last person, and stare at the concentric circles of tiny holes in the mouthpiece.

My mother's voice comes out of the other end, puny and hopeful. "Callie? Is that you?"

I hold my breath. There are kitchen sounds in the background, the thrum of the dishwasher, the closing of a drawer.

"Oh, dear," she says, the volume in her voice slipping down a notch, as if she were talking to herself. "How do I know if you're even there?"

My back stiffens; those were the same words the new girl used. I shift around on the little seat, then cough.

"Well, I hope you're there, Callie, because I have something to tell you." She waits a minute, then sighs. "OK. They say you're resisting treatment."

I switch the receiver to my other hand and wipe my palm on my pants leg.

"Oppositional something or other, they're calling it. Oppositional behavior."

Oppositional behavior. It sounds so premeditated, so on purpose.

"Are you listening?"

I forget not to nod—and forget my mom can't see me nodding.

"They say they might send you home."

The door frame of the tiny booth quivers. It narrows, then expands.

My mom is saying something about how the people at Sick Minds might want to give my bed to someone else. Someone who's willing to work. Someone who wants to get better.

The floor of the phone booth pitches up, then swims away.

Now she's saying something about school. "They won't let you back in school either," she says. "Not until you've had treatment."

I hold the receiver away from my ear. My mother's voice grows small, long-distance—*costing us good money . . . going to give your father a heart attack . . . don't understand why . . .* — until finally the phone goes dead and all that's left is a faint clicking in the wires.

The floor isn't where it's supposed to be when I step out of the phone booth; it's like when you step off a curb without knowing it and put your foot down into thin air. I grab the door frame, then force myself to walk back to my room. But the hall shimmers like a paved road on a hot summer day. Slick green squares of linoleum heave up in my path, then sink away underfoot. There's an incline, a linoleum hill, a surprisingly tiring hill that gives way, without warning, to a valley, a long, low trench in the hallway between the phone booth and my room.

The lights are out and Sydney's already in bed when I finally get there. I climb straight into bed and pull the blanket up to my chin even though I'm sweating from the walk back from the phone booth. My shirt and pants bunch up under the covers. I wrestle my shirt back into place, give up on the pants. I listen for Sydney's breathing. It's no good. I roll over; my shirt gets twisted around my chest. I turn back the other way and yank it straight.

I roll one way, the room rolls the other. I picture my bed, the bed that Sick Minds wants to give to someone else, falling through a giant trapdoor.

Then I hear Ruby's footsteps coming toward our door. The rolling stops, the furniture snaps back into place. Then she moves on.

Before the floor can start pitching again, I throw off the covers and crouch down next to the bed. I lift the mattress with one hand, grope around with the other. The mattress is surprisingly heavy. My arm shakes, bows under the weight of it. Then I feel it. Way down near the foot of the bed is the pie plate. I stretch, grab it, and let the mattress come down with a plop.

"Huh?" Sydney sits up in bed, her eyes half-open.

I freeze.

Sydney falls back onto her pillow, sighs, and settles into her steady breathing.

I get back into bed, moving calmly and efficiently now, lie on my stomach, and pull the covers over my head. Inside the dark blanket tent, I fold the pie plate in half, press it flat, bend it back and forth, back and forth, like I'm following a recipe, back and forth, until the fold is crisp. When I rip it, it gives way easily and I have two neat halves, each with a jagged edge.

I lay my index finger lightly on the edge of one half, testing it. It's rough and right.

I bring the inside of my wrist up to meet it. A tingle crawls across my scalp. I close my eyes and wait.

But nothing happens. There's no release. Just a weird tugging sensation. I open my eyes. The skin on my wrist is drawn up in a wrinkle, snagged on the edge. I pull it in the other direction and a dull throbbing starts in my wrist.

I hold my breath and push down on the piece of metal. It sinks in neatly.

A sudden liquid heat floods my body. The pain is so sharp, so sudden, I catch my breath. There's no rush, no relief. Just pain, a keen, pulsing pain. I drop the pie plate and grasp my wrist with my other hand, dimly aware even as I'm doing it that this is something I've never done before. Never tried to stop the blood. Never interfered. It's never hurt like this before. And it's never not worked.

I take my hand away a minute and wipe my wrist on my shirt; the blood pauses, then leaks out again. I go back to gripping my wrist and trying to ignore the throbbing and the pinpricks of sweat on my lip and forehead, then I look down and see blood seeping out between my fingers.

A sizzle of electricity, white-hot energy, courses through me. And suddenly I'm up, out of bed, walking out of the room. There's no thinking now, only walking. Down the hall, around the corner to Ruby's desk. Holding my arm out, like an offering.

"Oh, child," Ruby says when she sees me. "Oh, honey child."

She goes into action, reaching up to the First Aid cupboard and taking my hand in hers, all in one swift motion. She unwinds a roll of gauze, wipes away the blood, then washes the cut with some kind of solution. It burns, but for a moment at least, the throbbing lets up. I can see then that the cut isn't that deep, that it's no worse than the others, and I wonder why it bled so much, why I showed it to Ruby.

"It's a bleeder," she says, pressing a square of gauze to the cut. "But it's not deep. No need for stitches."

She closes both her hands around my wrist, as if she were praying, and pulls them to her chest, so close I can feel it rise and fall as she breathes. She presses with such a sure, steady force that after a while the bleeding stops and the pain begins to drain away.

She lowers my hand finally, puts another bandage over the cut, wraps gauze around my wrist with a dozen or so quick twists, and secures it with a couple of pieces of tape. We stand there a minute regarding her work. Then Ruby lowers herself into her chair, using one arm to support her weight. She drops into the chair with a sigh.

My body feels light all of a sudden, so light it might float off. I imagine myself as a giant Macy's Parade balloon, floating up, away from Ruby's desk, high over Sick Minds. I have to sit down.

Ruby leans forward, takes my hands in hers, and pulls them into her lap.

"Scared yourself, did you?" she says.

In the brown-black center of Ruby's eyes is a tiny, scared reflection of me.

"Why do you want to do a thing like that?" Our hands—ashy white and deep mahogany—are intertwined in Ruby's lap, the fabric of her dress soft from so many washings.

"Hmmm?" she says, as if I'd said something she hadn't quite heard. "Why don't you tell us what's bothering you?"

I consider pulling free of her grasp, but it would take too much effort and I'm tired now, very tired.

Ruby sighs. "Whatever it is, baby, it can't hurt worse than this."

Ruby walks me back to my room, her arm around my waist. This time, there's no question of how much distance to keep between us; I let myself sink against her. She tells me I'm lucky, that the cut wasn't deep, that I might have to get a tetanus shot, and that she'll have to file an incident report. "Standard operating procedure," she says. It occurs to me that I could be sent home or to Humdinger, and I wish Ruby would tell me one of her home truths or even just what standard operating procedure is, but when we get to my room she seems distracted. She lets go of my waist, reaches into the closet, and pulls out one of the nightgowns my mother bought.

"Put this on, child," she says. "And give me those clothes to wash. I'll be right out here waiting." She steps out into the hall.

I change into the nightgown, gather up my clothes, and start walking to the door to give them to Ruby. Something holds me in place halfway between the bed and the door, some vague sense that I'm forgetting something. Then I walk back to the bed, pick up the two jagged pieces of the pie plate, turn, and bring them to Ruby.

The green neon numbers on Sydney's alarm clock say 6:04 A.M. Last time I checked, it was 5:21. I brace myself on my arm and a dull pounding starts in my wrist. There, at the foot of the bed, is a neat bundle of clean, folded clothes. Ruby must have put them there before her shift ended.

I push back the covers, get up quietly, put on my clothes, and slip into the still-dark hallway. I tiptoe toward the bathroom, sneak past Marie's empty chair, past the phone booth, past the new girl's room, past the dayroom, the Group room, down the hall, past the Emergency Use Only door, until finally I'm sitting outside your office waiting for you to come to work.

I don't know how long I've been sitting here, but finally you're standing in front of me in your blue coat and scarf. You don't look surprised. You don't even say hello right away. You pull your keys out of your purse, bend down and turn on the UFO outside your door, and say, "Would you like to come in?"

I take my usual place on the couch while you hang up your coat and scarf, put your purse in a drawer, open the blinds. Finally you sit down.

"Callie?" you say. "Is there a reason why you're here?"

I shrug.

"Can you tell me what's on your mind?"

I start counting the stripes in the wallpaper. A dog barks in the distance. The sound rings in the air for a long time, then it's quiet.

"I can't." My voice surprises me. It's so puny.

54

"What? What is it you can't do?"

I clear my throat, but it doesn't do any good. Now there's no voice in there at all. I shrug.

"Callie." Your voice is firm. "Try to look at me."

I sneak a peek at you. Your eyes are amber. like Linus's. I look away.

"What is it you can't do?"

The radiator clicks on, drones for a while, clicks off.

"Talk." The word, finally, comes out of my mouth.

Your chair groans and I notice then that you've been sitting on the edge of your seat. You lean back and tap your lip with your finger, the way you did the other night in the game room.

"Is it because you're scared?"

I trace a square on the couch, nod yes, once, and watch, stunned, as a tear makes a small dark circle on my jeans.

You slide the tissue box across the carpet to me.

"Do you know why you're scared?"

I shake my head.

"Callie." Your voice comes at me from far away. "I think if we work really hard together, we may come up with some answers."

I rip the tissue in my hand. It's become a soggy useless mess. I grab another one.

"Would you like to try?"

I nod.

"Good." You sound pleased, really pleased.

I blow my nose. "What will you do to me?" The words seem to come out on their own.

You smile; tiny wrinkles fan out around your eyes and I wonder if maybe you're older than I thought. "*To* you? I won't do anything *to* you. We'll just talk."

"That's it?" My voice cracks. It's a weak, unreliable thing.

"That's it."

I grab another tissue from the box. "I feel . . ." I clear my throat and will the words to come out. "I feel like I'll be losing."

"Like a game or a contest?"

"Uh-huh."

"What do you think you'll lose?"

"I don't know." I check your amber cat eyes for signs of impatience, but you don't seem mad. Just curious.

"I'll never make you tell me anything you don't want to tell me," you say. "But you are right, Callie. Sometimes it will feel like you're losing something."

I reach for another tissue. Wet, wadded-up tissues keep piling up in my lap.

"But Callie," you say. "If we work hard, you'll find something much better to take the place of whatever you give up. I promise."

I nod. I'm tired now, awfully tired. I've got that headachy feeling I get in the summer when I step out of the dark, air-conditioned house into the too-bright sunlight.

I watch you as you stand up and say we'll get started later

on, at our usual time. Then you call for someone to escort me to the infirmary, where they give me a tetanus shot and make me sign a form. Then I go back to my room. And even though it's still morning, I go back to bed. And sleep. And sleep.

II

i must've slept all morning, because the next thing I know, Marie is shaking my shoulder and saying something about lunch. "C'mon," she says. "The doctor gave you special permission to be in your room unattended today, but now you've got to get up. Or else you're going to miss lunch."

I don't understand. Then it comes back to me, dimly at first, that something's different, although I can't remember exactly what it might be. I brush my hair out of my eyes and see a flash of white gauze around my wrist. In an instant, everything—my fingers gripping my wrist, Ruby folding her hands over mine, wet tissues heaped in my lap—comes back to me.

"We don't want you missing your meals," Marie says. She lowers her voice. "We got enough skinny girls in this place already."

I sit up and realize I'm hungry, really hungry.

• • •

Even the noise and the steamed-vegetable smell of the cafeteria doesn't spoil my appetite. I pick up a tray and let a cafeteria worker with fogged-up glasses shovel a grilled cheese sandwich onto my plate. I remember Sydney calling them chilled grease sandwiches once and I head out of the food line hoping she'll be there.

But the dining room is practically empty; the only ones left at our table are Debbie and Becca. I grip the edge of my tray and imagine myself walking past my usual seat at the end of the table, sitting down next to Debbie. I'll give her a practice smile, the way Ruth did, and start talking, like everybody else does. Debbie will say, "That's great, that's really great," the way she does when Becca eats all of her fruit and cottage cheese, and Becca will be impressed, she'll agree with Debbie that it's great, and when we go to Group later on, she'll run ahead and tell everyone the news. But before I even get to the table, they've left.

A few minutes later, Tara comes in and sets her tray down at the other end of the table. Her nose is red and her face is blotchy and as soon as she sees me watching her she pulls the brim of her baseball cap down. She picks up a piece of lettuce and wipes the dressing off with her napkin.

Finally I stand and pick up my tray, keeping my sleeve pulled down over my wrist, the hem wrapped around my thumb, and sit down across from her.

"Hi," she says.

I try to give her a practice smile, but I'm not sure anything happens on my face.

Then we both sit there pretending to eat. I try to remember how people start conversations, but all that comes to mind are phrases from sixth-grade French. "Bonjour, Thérèse. Ça va?" says Guy, a boy wearing a black beret. "Ça va bien, merci. Et tu, Guy?" Thérèse responds.

I decide to take a sip of water and then just say hi. Hi. It's just two little letters. I ought to be able to get that much out. I reach for my glass. My sleeve creeps up and we both see the white bandage sticking out. The water in my glass jumps as I pull my hand away and tuck it safely in my lap.

"Oh" is all she says.

I peek out at her from under my bangs.

"You really don't understand, do you?" Her voice is gentle, the way it was in the bathroom the day she asked if I wanted her to leave me alone.

I shake my head.

"We all do things."

"Where would you like to start?" you say that afternoon.

I notice that you're wearing your delicate little fabric shoes again today.

"Callie? Why don't you tell me about things before you came here?"

"Don't you—" My voice deserts me. "Don't you know?"

You tap your pen against something in your lap; I see then that you didn't throw my file away after all.

"No," you say. "I don't. All this tells me is what other people have to say about you."

I squint at the folder, wondering who these other people are and what they have to say.

You open the folder, then close it. "That you're fifteen, a runner—"

"Was."

"Pardon me?"

"I was." I cough. "A runner."

You pick up your pen.

"Are you going to write everything down?"

"Not if you don't want me to." You hold your pen in midair. "Will it bother you if I take notes?"

I shrug.

"If it bothers you, I won't."

For some reason, I think of how Mr. Malcolm, my algebra teacher, used to hand out test papers with lots of blank space and tell us we wouldn't get credit for right answers unless we showed our work. I imagine you working on me as an algebra problem, reducing me to fractions, crossing out common denominators, until there's nothing left on the page but a line that says x = whatever it is that is wrong with me. You fix it. I get to go home.

"Would you rather I didn't take notes?"

"It's OK." You bend over your notepad a little; I study the part in your hair, which is perfectly straight and tidy. You straighten up. "So, where do you want to start?"

I shrug.

You wait.

"I don't care," I say.

You cross your legs, not taking your eyes off me. The minute hand on the clock twitches forward once, then once more.

"My little brother, Sam," I say finally. "He's the one who usually gets all the attention from doctors and stuff."

Instantly, this sounds wrong.

"I don't mind," I say. "He's sick."

"What's the matter with Sam?"

"Asthma."

You don't say anything.

"Really bad asthma."

You don't move.

"He's in the hospital all the time."

You still don't move.

"That's why he's so skinny and why we have to keep everything clean. But he's OK for a brother." I know I'm supposed to say more, but I'm exhausted, out of words. "That's all, I guess."

You fold your hands in your lap. "What's that like for you?"

"What?"

"Having a brother who needs so much attention."

"I'm used to it."

You open your mouth to say something, but I cut you off.

"My mom's the one who has a hard time."

"Your mom?"

"She worries a lot."

"What does she worry about?"

I try to get comfortable on the couch. This is tiring, all this talking.

"Callie," you say. "What does your mother worry about?"

"Everything."

You look like you want to ask something else, so I go on.

"She doesn't drive anymore. She's terrified of trucks. My dad has to take us everywhere."

"I see."

I wonder if you do see, see us sitting in the car, strapped in our seats, the windows rolled up tight, even if it's a nice day, especially if it's a nice day, so no pollen or spores or dust mites or pollution or anything can get into our car, our quiet, anti-septic car.

"Can you tell me about that?"

"About what?"

"About the times Sam was in the hospital."

I blink. Were we talking about the times Sam was in the hospital? Or did you say something and I missed it? I pinch the edge of my bandage, tugging ever so slightly. A single, sterile white thread comes unraveled.

"Like what? What do you want me to tell you?"

"Well, what do you do when your parents are with Sam?"

I roll the thin piece of thread into a tiny, tiny ball.

"I don't know. Clean."

You don't say anything. The ball is microscopic now.

"I dust. Wash things. Vacuum. We have to vacuum a lot."

You still don't say anything. The ball is so tiny I lose it.

"Clean the lint filters. We have special filters on all the air

63

vents because of Sam. One time I organized all my mom's coupons. That's it. Boring stuff."

There's a long silence. I feel around for the ball, listen to the hum of the UFO, check the clock.

"Sometimes if they have to stay over, I watch TV."

"What do you watch?"

"Um. I don't know. The Food Channel. . . . *Rescue 911*."

"Why do you like those shows?"

"I don't know."

The minute hand lurches forward again while you wait for me to come up with a better answer.

"*Rescue 911* . . ." you say. "Is there something in particular you like about that show?"

I shrug. "No." Then, "Yeah, I guess. I don't know."

You raise an eyebrow.

"I guess it's because . . . I guess usually when people get saved it's because some little kid is the one that notices that something's wrong. Or the dog. Or a neighbor."

You write something in your notebook.

"There's always a happy ending; after the person gets rescued, everything turns out OK."

I listen to the traffic, far away on the highway, and I study a crack in your ceiling. Like the crack in the ceiling of the hospital where Madeline went to have her appendix taken out, this one also has the habit of sometimes looking like a rabbit. I rhyme *habit* and *rabbit* in my head over and over until I can't tell which came first—the habit or the rabbit.

"How long has Sam had asthma?"

Your voice startles me. I'd almost forgotten you were there.

"What?"

"When did Sam develop asthma?"

I jump, the way I always did at a track meet when the ref would cock the starting gun and yell, "On your mark."

"Callie?"

My thigh muscles are twitching, my feet are sweating. I press my hands to my legs to still them. It's no good. "A year ago, maybe a little more." I try to sound casual, bored even.

"A year ago," you repeat.

I slide forward on the couch, ready to go.

"And while your parents were at the hospital, who took care of you?"

I'm sitting on the edge of the couch now. "I take care of myself."

You uncross your legs, cap your pen, and say I did good work. I check the clock. Our time was up five minutes ago.

On the way back from your office I pass the dayroom. The TV voice of a talk-show host competes with the *tick-tock* of a Ping-Pong game. I tuck my head down and slink by. As I pass the door, a tiny white ball skitters out into the hallway and rolls to a stop at my feet.

"Hey, S.T.," Sydney calls out. "Bring it here, will you?"

I consider the ball at my feet, then Sydney's flushed, happy face.

"Please?" She smiles a wide smile.

I bend and pick it up. It's like picking up air, it's so light. I take baby steps across the hall, then into the dayroom, eyeing the ball every second, watching it wobble back and forth in my open palm, waiting for it to fall out of my hand and bounce down the hall, out the front door.

Sydney plucks the ball out of my hand. "Thanks," she says over her shoulder.

My palm is suddenly empty. I don't know what I'm supposed to do next.

Sydney notices. "Wanna play?" She holds out her paddle.

I scan the room. Debbie and Becca are sitting on the armchair, Debbie in the chair, Becca perched on the arm. Tiffany's at the other end of the table, holding a paddle, still wearing her purse. Tara's standing by the chalkboard, keeping score.

"You can just watch if you want," says Sydney. She gestures to an empty chair.

"Please," says Tara.

Walking across the room to the empty chair seems like it would take a lot of steps. The door is much closer. I shake my head and turn to go, knowing, even as I walk away, that I was wrong. Getting to the door takes forever.

"Where would you like to start today?" you say.

I consider. "With Sam. Could we talk about Sam some more?"

"Sure."

But I can't think of what to say about Sam.

66

"Did I tell you about his hockey cards?"

You shake your head.

"He has this huge collection of cards. He gets a new pack whenever he gets sick. He loves those cards. He sorts them into piles all the time."

You don't say anything.

"According to teams or positions or statistics or whatever."

You don't move. I trace a triangle on the couch.

"My mom sits there with him after school. At the breakfast nook. She tats."

You tilt your head to the side. "Tats?"

I stop tracing. "Tatting. It's where you make lacy things like doilies and angels and things out of string. She tats and he sorts."

Telling you about my mom and Sam at home in the breakfast nook feels wrong somehow, private.

"They have to take it easy," I explain. "They have to rest a lot."

"What do you do?"

"What do I do?"

"While your mother tats and your brother sorts, what do you do?"

"Oh." I trace and retrace the triangle, stop, then start again. "Nothing. Watch TV."

You wait for me to say more.

"I keep it on mute if they're resting."

You wrinkle your brow.

"I can read the captions if my mom and Sam are resting."

"You watch the TV on mute?"

"I'm good at it."

You shake your head slightly. "I don't understand, exactly."

I picture the big soundless TV in our family room, subtitles scrolling by at the foot of the screen. "The words at the bottom, they're always a few seconds behind what the people on TV are saying. I can usually predict what they're going to say."

You seem like you're going to ask a question.

"It's kind of like a hobby," I say.

You write in your notebook. "Do you have any other hobbies?"

"Not really." I button my sweater. I unbutton it.

"What about running?" you say.

I can see myself running—not my whole self, just my feet beneath me, each one appearing, then disappearing, then reappearing, over and over and over. "What about it?" I say.

"Well, what does it feel like when you run?"

"I don't know." I pick at a hangnail. "I don't feel much."

You tap your finger to your lip.

"That's sort of why I like it."

Your dead-cow chair creaks. You lean forward and open your mouth to speak.

"My mom never liked it," I say. "She always thought I was going to get hit by a car or something."

You sit back.

"She said she was always waiting to get a call from the police," I say. "Whenever I came in from running, she looked sort of mad."

I picture my mom sitting in the breakfast nook, tatting and frowning, while Sam deals out his hockey cards in neat piles. She doesn't look up when I come in, she just keeps tatting. Sam shows me his cards, pictures of hockey players smiling, hockey players skating, players with their helmets on, with their helmets off. "Don't you want to take a shower?" my mom says. "Don't you have some homework to do?"

You're staring at me intently; you must have asked me a question.

"What?"

"I'm not sure I understand," you say. "Why would your mother be angry at you?"

"I don't know. As soon as I come in she always says 'Don't you have some homework to do?' So I usually just go upstairs and leave them alone."

Your eyes widen slightly. "Is that how it feels?"

"What?"

"That your mother doesn't want you around so she can be alone with your brother?"

I don't know how exactly, but somehow I've said something I didn't mean to say. Something that's not quite true. Or maybe something that's sort of a little bit true.

I spend the rest of the hour staring down the clock.

• • •

Study Hall is a completely different place at night. Everybody has to be there from seven till eight, since we all have to keep up with our schoolwork during our stay at Sick Minds. We're supposed to be silent, but people whisper and pass notes all the time; whenever the attendant steps out, the room erupts.

Right now, though, it's quiet. Tara's painting her nails, Tiffany's writing a letter to a friend out in the real world, Becca's asleep, and Debbie's tracing a magazine picture of a model in a ball gown. Only Sydney is actually doing homework.

The new girl, whose name is apparently Amanda—I checked the chalkboard—is stretched out in a chair in the last row, doing an imitation of being asleep. Her head is leaning against the wall, her eyes are closed, her mouth is curled in a half-smile. I know she's awake, though, because I can see her bumping the inside of her wrist against the edge of the chair in a rhythmic motion.

Watching her bugs me, so I go back to my French assignment, which is to memorize vocabulary words that might come in handy on vacation, words for things like bikinis, rental cars, and restaurants. Since we aren't allowed to use pencils here, even for math (they're considered "sharps"), I have to write with a felt-tip pen, which smears; I crumple the page and start again.

The attendant gets up and says she's going to take her

empty soda can to the recycling bin down the hall. She says she expects us all to behave.

She leaves; instantly, the room comes to life.

"Can I have the nail polish when you're done?" Sydney asks Tara.

"If I can borrow your Walkman," says Tara.

While they're busy making the switch, Tiffany turns around to check out Debbie's drawing. Debbie cups her hand over it, too late.

"Why do you do that all the time?" Tiffany says to Debbie.

"Do what?"

"Draw pictures of thin people?"

The attendant comes back, clearing her throat loudly. Tiffany whips around in her seat; everyone goes back to what they were doing.

Debbie's stunned. She pulls back the tracing paper and studies the model in the magazine. Then she thumbs through her notebook. Pictures of tall, slender women in fancy clothes go by. She gets to the last page and looks up. No one sees but me. Debbie has tears in her eyes.

I turn away, quickly, but Debbie knows I saw. When I look back a few seconds later, she's draping her sweater over Becca, tucking the fabric around her, the way a mother would. When I first got here, Debbie tried to talk to me; she even offered me a piece of cake her mother sent her. By now, though, I've probably scared her away.

71

Debbie pulls the sweater up around Becca's neck, which is unbelievably white and fragile, closes her notebook, and stares into space until the attendant says we can go.

Rochelle, the bathroom attendant, is bent over her magazine when I go in to brush my teeth that night. Someone in the toilet stall behind me jiggles the handle. The toilet wheezes, then roars. The sour smell of vomit fills the air.

Becca comes out of the stall, wearing a bathrobe with puppies printed on it and brown furry slippers that are actually shaped like puppies. The stall door bangs in her wake. Then her face is next to mine in the mirror. She dabs the corner of her mouth with toilet paper.

As Becca breezes out, I watch Rochelle out of the corner of my eye. Her lips are moving as she reads; she doesn't even register Becca going by.

Amanda's missing at breakfast the next day. This is a big deal because meals are mandatory, even if you're not a food-issues person. Debbie's gone over to the cafeteria attendant to find out what's going on.

"Debbie should butt out," says Tiffany.

"She's just trying to help," says Becca.

Tiffany rolls her eyes; I run my finger along the metal strip at the edge of the table and notice that it's ever so slightly loose.

The chimes sound; breakfast is over. There's a lot of clattering and complaining as people nearby get up to go wherever they're going. Our group stalls, waiting for Debbie. She hurries back to our table and everyone leans in to hear what she has to say.

"She got caught," Debbie whispers. "Cutting."

My cheeks flame, I pull my sleeves down and stare at my lap.

"Eeuww," says Becca. "That's so gross."

"Shut up," says Sydney. I don't look up, but I think she said that for my sake. "So where is she?"

"Hammacher, probably," says Debbie.

"How do you know?" says Sydney.

"I heard she had to get a shot," says Debbie. She lowers her voice dramatically. "A sedative."

The cafeteria attendant comes over and tells us we better get moving, that she's handing out demerits today. We gather up our trays and head toward the dishroom. I'm by myself, as usual, tagging along behind Tiffany and Sydney.

"They say *we're* nuts because we like to get wasted," Tiffany says, shaking her head. "What that new girl, Amanda, what she does is crazy."

Sydney turns around to see if I've heard; I turn back to the breakfast table, pretending I've forgotten something. Getting a demerit for being late would be better than having to see the worried look on Sydney's face.

You sit down in your chair, a fresh sheet of paper at the ready.

"I don't feel like talking today," I say.

You nod. "All right," you say.

We sit there a while, me studying a shaft of weak winter sunlight, you studying a file.

"Is that mine?" I say.

"Yes."

I go back to looking at the patch of sun; I decide it's a rhomboid. "What's it say?"

"Your file? Not a lot."

I sit very still.

"There's some basic information about you, an intake evaluation, a school report."

A cloud passes by outside; the rhomboid disappears.

"Who wrote the school report?" I say.

You open the file. "A Miss Magee," you say. "The school nurse."

"She was a sub."

"Oh."

Sun pours in through the window again; the rhomboid is now just a basic parallelogram.

"She was the one who discovered that you were cutting your arms, wasn't she?"

"She called me sweetie," I say. Immediately I wish I hadn't said this.

"Sweetie?"

"Never mind."

I look for the rabbit crack on the ceiling, but I can't quite find it.

"She wore socks and sandals," I say.

"What else do you remember?"

"She said her regular job was at a drug rehab. She said, 'We let it all hang out there.' She was sort of a hippie."

You wait to see if I'll say more.

"I used to get these stomach aches. The regular nurse always sent me back to class."

"And this substitute nurse? This Miss Magee?"

"She said, 'Is something bothering you, sweetie?'"

You smile ever so slightly.

"I just kept staring at the eye chart behind her after that. I can still remember the first line: E F S P D."

You smile a little more.

"She made me sit on the examining table. She felt my forehead. She took my pulse. Then she dropped my arm and said, 'Oh, wow.' She said she'd be right back. I lay down on the table and the next thing I remember, she was shaking my shoulder to wake me up. My mom was standing there, pressing a tissue to her lips."

I check to see if you are pleased with all these words. You look concerned.

"You know what?" I say. "I've thought about her a lot since I've been here."

You tilt your head.

"About . . . what's her name?" I say. "The substitute nurse."

"Shelly Magee."

"Yeah. I've thought about sending her a postcard."

75

You raise an eyebrow.

"You know—'Having a wonderful time. Wish you were here.'"

"Are you?"

I don't understand.

"Are you having a wonderful time?"

I pick a piece of fuzz off the couch, roll it between my fingers, flick it into the air.

"Do you wish she was here?"

"No."

"Callie, let me ask you something." You sit forward in your dead-cow chair. "How exactly did Shelly Magee see your scars?"

"She took my pulse."

"You didn't try to stop her?"

A sudden heat washes over me. I can feel my cheeks reddening, my throat getting tight. I pull my arms to my sides and sit very still.

"I'm glad you didn't try to stop her." Your voice comes across the space between us, gentle but sure.

I take in the sight of you in your leather chair, so calm, so normal, so pretty in your long green skirt.

"You don't think I'm crazy?" I laugh.

You don't laugh.

"You don't think I'm insane for doing this?" I hold up my arm, my sleeve pulled safely over my bandage.

"No, Callie," you say matter-of-factly. "I don't think you're crazy at all."

I blink.

"I think you've come up with a way to deal with feelings that you find overwhelming. Overwhelmingly bad, overwhelmingly frightening."

I sink back into the cushions on your couch. It occurs to me that I sit up perfectly straight the whole time I'm in here, that my back has never actually touched the back of the couch.

"Really?" I say.

"Really."

The clock says it's time to go.

"So, can you make me stop?" I say.

"Make you? No. I can't make you."

"Well, then, can you, you know, help?"

You tap your lip. "Yes," you say, "if you want to stop." Then you stand up and say we'll talk more tomorrow.

I say OK, but what I really want to say is that I'm not sure I *can* stop.

Everyone else must still be on the smoking porch because Claire's the only one in the room when I get to Group. Her glasses are in her hands and she's pinching the bridge of her nose; there are two red spots where her glasses usually sit. She looks up when she sees me at the door and smiles. I don't exactly smile back, but I don't not smile either. We sit there a while, me reviewing the new order of cars in the parking lot and Claire blowing on coffee in a paper cup, until the other girls file in.

The room is suddenly full of talking and laughing. Sydney is at the end of one of her stories. "That *proves* I'm the sanest one in the family," she says, flopping down in her chair.

"Me too!" Tara practically cries out. Then she stops cold in the center of the circle: Amanda is back and she's sitting in Tara's seat.

Tara gives Claire a pleading look. Claire doesn't respond; Sydney pats the seat of the chair next to hers, and Tara slips in beside Sydney.

Suddenly Group is a game of musical chairs. Tiffany comes in, surveys the situation, looks to Claire for help, then plunks into the nearest seat. Becca and Debbie arrive last.

Becca darts into the seat next to Tara. Debbie huffs, then takes the last seat, the one next to me.

I draw my arms to my side to make room for her.

There's a long silence. Somebody complains about the food. Then more silence. Somebody else complains about the bathrooms then about how nosy the attendants are. More silence.

"So?" Sydney says to Amanda. "Where were you?"

"When?"

Sydney looks around the group for help.

"At breakfast," Tara says. "You weren't at breakfast."

Amanda smirks. "Room service."

Tiffany laughs. No one else does.

"Seriously," says Sydney.

"You really care?" says Amanda. "That's so co-dependent of you."

Sydney looks confused, then hurt.

"I was in the infirmary," Amanda says.

"Really?" says Debbie.

"Really," Amanda says sarcastically.

"I heard you had to get a shot," Debbie says.

Amanda arches an eyebrow.

"Didn't they give you a sedative?" says Debbie.

Amanda laughs. "Tetanus," she announces. Then she leans forward and winks at me. "Right?"

I can't answer, but I can't stand to have everybody looking at me either. I nod. Then I go back to looking out the window and wondering whatever happened to that fly that was caught between the glass and the screen.

After Group, Ruby waves to me from her desk. "You have a package," she says. "Priority Mail."

I know, as soon as I see it, it's from my mother. The mailing box is covered with cat stickers, the address is written in calligraphy; I wonder what the Sick Minds postman must have thought.

I tuck it under my arm and start to head back to my room.

"Hold on," says Ruby. "You have to open that under supervision. Standard operating procedure."

Ruby uses a key to slice through the mailing tape. Inside,

nestled in a sea of pink Styrofoam peanuts, is a quilted calico thing. She holds it up. It's my name, in puffy calico letters.

On the back is a suction cup. She hands me a note that was lying among the peanuts.

Dear Callie,

Here's a little something to brighten your room at Sea Pines. The suction cup on the back is so you can hang it on your door. (I checked with the office, since you girls aren't allowed to have thumbtacks.) Let me know if the other girls would like them. I can make them up in a jiffy.

They said you're doing better there. That's good. Get well soon.

Love,
Mom

I take the calico name thing and start to walk back to my room.

"Wait," says Ruby. "There's something else."

I try to act like I don't care what it is, like I'm not interested, like I'm not hoping for anything good, anything from my dad, as Ruby hands me a small white envelope.

I know as soon as I see the front, with my name in blue marker, it's from Sam. Inside is a hockey card. Not just any card, though, it's his Wayne Gretzky, his favorite. There's no note, just the card.

I check to make sure no one's around. Then I hold the

card up so Ruby can see. "My little brother," I say. "He loves hockey."

She puts a hand to her chest. "That's sweet," she says. "Real sweet."

I slip Wayne Gretzky into my pocket and go back to my room.

"Where would you like to start today?" you say.

"I don't care."

You cross your legs.

"You decide," I say.

"OK," you say. "How are you getting along with the other girls in your group?"

I shrug. "Fine."

You wait.

"Sydney, my roommate, she's nice," I say. "So is this other girl, Tara."

You look pleased.

"And Debbie, she's this very heavy girl who's kind of a know-it-all, but she's OK. She tries to take care of this other girl, Becca."

"Hmm," is all you say.

"I'm not sure about Becca. She got so sick from not eating she had a heart attack. She acts like she wants to get better, but—"

"But . . ."

"Never mind."

I wait for you to bug me to go on. You don't.

"You won't tell anyone, right?" I say.

"Everything you say in here is confidential."

"Well, she . . . I . . . she's still throwing up her food."

Your expression doesn't change.

"And hiding food, too. She pretends to eat it, but she's really throwing it away."

You uncross your legs. "How do you know?"

"I watch."

You nod.

"It makes me feel sort of weird that I know what she's doing. It also makes me feel really bad for Debbie, since Debbie does nice things for her like covering her up with a sweater when she's sleeping."

Talking about Debbie and Becca and Sydney and Tara is surprisingly easy. I realize I know a lot about them; I guess I even sort of like them. I check the clock to see how long it is till lunch.

Your chair groans. "But I understand from the staff here that you're not talking in Group yet."

Yet. You say this like it's simple, inevitable. My lips are chapped; I pull the corner of my lower lip into my mouth, then bite down a little.

"Can you tell me why?"

I shrug, for the millionth time.

You tap your lip.

"There's this other girl," I say. "She's new."

"Oh?"

"This new girl, Amanda, she wears shorts and flip-flops . . ."

You lift an eyebrow, ever so slightly.

". . . like it's the middle of summer."

There's a long, long hush. Far off, I can hear a plane boring through the sky.

"She does what I do."

I watch for your expression to change, for there to be some slight shift from neutral to . . . to what? Disgusted? Disapproving? You wait calmly.

"She showed everybody her scars."

I bite my lip some more. That's it. I'm finished. I listen for the plane, but it's gone.

"You think she should have kept them to herself?"

"Huh?"

"Do you think this new girl should have kept her scars hidden?"

"I don't care." Then, right away, "They're gross."

I pull on my sleeve, pinch the fabric tight, wrap it safely around my thumb.

"What's wrong with letting people know what you're doing, or how you're feeling?"

"It's not fair," I say.

"Not fair?"

"It might upset them."

You look puzzled.

"Can we change the subject?" I say.

"Of course."

But I can't think of what to talk about.

"My mom sent me this name thing," I say at last. "I told you she does crafts, right?"

You nod.

"She made this thing for my door. It's my name. In fabric. It's quilted."

The name thing seems silly, impossible to describe.

"It's a decoration?" you say.

"Yeah, I guess."

"Mm-hmm."

"My mom has to take it easy," I explain.

"Yes," you say. "You mentioned that before. That she needs a lot of rest."

All at once, though, I'm the one who feels tired. Exhausted, actually.

"Is it OK if we stop now?" I say.

"Yes, of course," you say, smiling a little. "Our time is just about up anyway."

It's almost the end of Study Hall. Debbie's writing in her journal. Sydney's listening to her Walkman. Everyone else is asleep. I'm memorizing chemistry terms: osmosis, reverse osmosis.

Sydney leans across the space between our desks, waving a folded note. She points to Tara. I know right away she wants me to pass the note to Tara; I take it without thinking.

84

Then I see the problem. Tara is sound asleep, her head on her arms, turned away from me.

I watch Tara breathing for a minute, try to decide what to do, then lean across the row and slide the note under her elbow. She doesn't move. I look over at Sydney, who's giggling silently, her hand over her mouth. The corners of my mouth turn up; I bite down on the insides of my cheeks and turn back toward Tara.

I reach over and slip the note out from under Tara's elbow. She still doesn't move. Sydney is practically having a convulsion trying not to laugh; her face is beet red. My chest feels like it's about to explode. I swallow, then burst out with a noise that sounds like air escaping from a balloon.

Tara jumps. Sydney laughs out loud, like this is the funniest thing she's ever seen. All I know is that my hand is shaking as I pass Tara the note.

"Thanks," Sydney whispers.

"Sure," I say. *Sure*. It's the kind of thing that comes out automatically. The kind of thing a person can say without really saying anything.

I close the door to your office; before you can ask me what I want to talk about, I show you the Wayne Gretzky card.

"It's Sam's favorite," I say.

You smile. "You told me how much he loves those cards," you say.

I sit back on the couch; my feet stick out. I sit forward; my

85

back gets tight. "Yeah, but he doesn't actually play. He just looks at the cards."

You nod.

"He has this tabletop hockey game. I set it up for him. It has plastic players that you control with sticks, you know?"

I can't tell if you understand what I'm talking about, but the words keep coming anyhow.

"He got it the Christmas before last. It had about ten pages of directions. Stuff like 'Put bracket X in slot Z, post Y in hole 22.'"

"Sounds complicated," you say.

"Yeah, the box said 'Adult assembly required.' But my parents were out. My mom was visiting Gram at the nursing home."

"So you put it together by yourself?"

"No big deal." This sounds somehow like bragging, so I tell you the rest. "I got mad at Sam, though. I hardly ever get mad at Sam."

You tilt your head to the side.

"He put the stickers on crooked." This sounds stupid, trivial. "The directions say that's the last thing you're supposed to do."

"And that made you angry?"

"Maybe. A little," I say. Then, "I was mean."

"How were you mean?" You sound faintly disbelieving, like you can't imagine me being mean.

"I yelled at him."

I check for your reaction. You just look calm, as usual.

"He got sick." I let the words fall in my lap, then look up. You nod.

"He had to go to the hospital," I say.

You give me a worried look; I want to make it go away.

"You know what Sam said? He still believed in Santa. He said he was mad at Santa for not putting the hockey game together. I said maybe Santa was too busy. So Sam said, 'That's what he has elves for.'" I smile, thinking how funny that was coming from a little kid.

You smile a little, too. I decide to tell you more.

"He put the stickers on when I wasn't looking. They were all wrinkled. And he put the stickers that were supposed to go on the players' uniforms on the scoreboard. I told him he was wrecking the whole thing. He hid the rest of the stickers behind his back, and then he started to cry."

I don't check for your reaction; I keep my eyes on the rabbit and go on.

"I didn't pay any attention. I kept working on the hockey game. He kept crying, though. Then he pulled on my sleeve and said he couldn't breathe. His eyes were really big and he made this scary noise, this wet sound that came from his chest, like he was drowning from the inside."

I rip the tissue in my lap and decide to skip over the other part.

"They took him to the hospital. It was after midnight when they got home—"

"Excuse me a minute, Callie." You're leaning forward in your chair. "Who took him to the hospital?"

"My parents." I glance at you, then away.

"So they came home?" You look confused.

"Yeah." I go on, faster. "It was after midnight when they got home, 12:12 in the morning. I remember. I decided that if they weren't home by 12:34 I was going to call the hospital to see if Sam was OK. You know how on a digital clock 12:34 looks like 1-2-3-4? That was going to be the sign that I should call." I don't wait to see if you understand. "But they came home, so I didn't have to."

You exhale.

"My mom was upset. She wanted to know why I wasn't in bed. She said Sam was in an oxygen tent. Then she started crying and it was like her legs gave out; she was kneeling on the floor, crying and saying, 'Oh my God, oh my God.' My dad had to pick her up under the arms and put her to bed."

I check the clock. Time's up, somehow. I squirm around on the couch. You don't move. I inch to the edge of the couch. You still don't move.

"That must have been very upsetting," you say.

I stand up. "Yeah. For my mom. She told someone on the phone Sam almost died. It was after that, she stopped driving and stuff."

I put my hand on the doorknob. "That's it," I say.

I don't wait for you. I open the door and say, "See you to-morrow."

That night when I go to take my shower, Becca's standing at the sink wearing her puppy bathrobe and slippers. Until a while ago, I thought Becca was about my age. Then the other day in Group, when she told us they tried to force-feed her when she was in the hospital, she said they couldn't do it because she was legally an adult. "No one can tell me what to do," she said. "I'm eighteen years old."

She's holding a toothbrush and scowling at her reflection. Then, as if she's just remembered she was in the middle of something, she starts brushing her teeth so hard it looks like it must hurt.

I head toward a sink at the other end, aware of the distinct smell of throw-up as I pass one of the stalls. Becca is spraying herself with perfume. Rochelle is oblivious.

I position myself so I can see Becca in the mirror. She catches me looking at her; we lock eyes for an instant. She looks embarrassed and proud at the same time. I grab my towel, pretend I forgot something in my room, and decide to come back later.

"I don't have anything to say today," I say as I sit down on your couch.

"No?"

"No. Not really."

"Let me ask you something, then," you say.

You don't wait to see if it's OK with me.

"The time Sam got sick, when you were putting together the hockey set—is there anything else you want to tell me about it?"

I study a stain on the carpet and try to decide if it's shaped like a woman with a big nose or an amoeba. "It was raining," I say finally.

"Anything else?"

I don't take my eyes off the stain. "Nope."

"Well then, will you fill me in on one part I don't understand?" You keep going. "Your parents were out, as I recall. Is that right?"

I don't move a muscle.

"How did you let them know Sam was sick? Do you remember?"

I remember exactly.

I took the steps up from the basement two at a time, then ran out the front door, across the lawn, into the street. I glanced back at our house with all my mom's Christmas crafts in the windows, then tried to put on a burst of speed. I stumbled, pitched forward, and found myself kneeling by the curb. I don't remember getting up, I just remember running, watching my feet beneath me, first one, then the other, hitting the pavement as if they weren't connected to me, as if they were just appearing and disappearing to give me something to look at while I ran.

I ran past the entrance to our development, out onto the main road. I must have gone past the Roy Rogers, the Dairy Queen, and the video rental place, although I don't remember going past them. I just watched my feet appear, disappear, then reappear until somehow I was standing in front of Bud's Tavern. I shoved the door open and stepped inside, but

I couldn't see a thing in the sudden dark. The place smelled like overcooked hot dogs and damp sweaters; I thought for a minute I was going to be sick.

There was a man at the bar. "Daddy!" I said. It came out sounding babyish and a little scared. The man turned around and gave me a bored look; he wasn't my father. Another man came out of the restroom, whistling. "Daddy!" This time it sounded babyish and a little mad. And this time it was my father.

He looked like he couldn't quite place me. "Callie?" he said. "What are you doing here?"

"It's Sam," I said, panting. "He's sick."

"You want a soda?" he said, then turned to face the bar; his back looked enormous. When he turned around, he had a beer in his hand. He took a swallow and I watched his Adam's apple bob up, then down.

"He's sick!"

He looked at me blankly.

"Daddy!" I stamped my foot. "I already called mom at the nursing home," I said quietly. "She's on her way home."

He seemed to wake up then. "Why didn't you say so?" He took out his wallet, put a few bills on the counter, and grabbed his coat.

Once we got in the car, I realized I was cold. Cold and wet. "Could you put on the heat?" I said.

He didn't say anything, just flipped the heater on. It blew out cold air at first and I had to hug my arms to my side to keep from getting even colder. When the car started to warm up, he turned the heater off, unzipped his coat, and tugged on his collar.

All the things I'd passed on my way there—the fast-food places, the video rental store—went by the window in slow motion. How could it take so much longer to drive home than it had to run there? But it must have just seemed slow, because we still got there before my mom did.

I remember exactly, but I don't tell you. I just sit there and stare at the stain on the carpet until finally you sigh and say that's all the time we have for today.

Something wakes me up in the middle of the night: the quiet. I sit up, listen for the squeaking of Ruby's shoes, for the sound of someone crying into a pillow, for the far-off laugh track from the attendants' TV. But for once it's absolutely silent in here. The room is filled with a milky white glow; I sit up and see then that it's snowing. I listen to the snowflakes hitting the window, making a faint scratching sound. Then I lie down, roll over, try to go back to sleep. In the distance, car tires spin, then stop.

I remember a talk show about people who had trouble falling asleep; some expert told them to get up and read or have a glass of milk instead of trying to sleep. Still, I try to sleep. I play the inhale-exhale game. It doesn't work. Finally I get up, feel around for my slippers, and decide to see if Ruby's at the desk knitting or something.

Outside each dorm room, near the floor, are a pair of

childproof night-lights; I think about telling Ruby that this makes the hallway look like an airport landing strip. She'll like that. We'll talk. After that, I'll be able to sleep.

Down at the end of the hall, Rochelle is at her post, on the lookout for late-night barfers and illegal laxative users. As I pass Becca's room, something in the dim glow of the night-light catches my eye. It's Ruby, sitting on the edge of Becca's bed. I decide to wait for her so I can tell her about the landing strip.

Ruby glances up, gives me a half-worried, half-annoyed look; I shrink back against the wall, then tiptoe back to my room and count the snowflakes until, somehow, it's morning and Sydney's making her bed.

The cafeteria is more insane than usual. Maybe it's the snow, maybe it's the pancakes; the clatter and the laughing and the talking are worse than ever. I'm in line, waiting for my breakfast, when Debbie cuts in front of me. She's apparently back for seconds; an empty, syrup-streaked plate is in her hand.

"What's taking so long?" she yells over the counter to a kitchen worker in a hair net.

The woman smiles nervously; Debbie hands her plate across the counter.

"I need more," she says.

By the time I get my juice and sit down, Debbie's almost finished. Tara's sitting across from her, watching, practically terrified, as Debbie eats one mouthful of pancake after another. Amanda regards Debbie with something like awe.

"Where's Becca?" Sydney says.

No one answers; Debbie keeps chewing as if she hasn't heard.

"Deb?" says Sydney. "Where's Becca?"

"Infirmary." Debbie sounds bored, matter-of-fact; she doesn't look at Sydney, she stares at some spot on the far wall.

Tara sets her juice glass down slowly. "What's the matter with her?"

Debbie doesn't answer; she chews, scoops up another piece, pops it in her mouth.

"Debbie?" Tara looks like she's going to cry.

"Debbie!" says Sydney. "What's wrong?"

She shrugs.

"Is it her heart?" Tara says.

Debbie gets to her feet hurriedly. Her lower lip is quivery. "I don't know." She grabs her tray and storms away.

Our table goes quiet. Then there's a flurry of talking.

"I bet it's another heart attack," Tara says.

Sydney drapes an arm around Tara's shoulders. "Don't worry," she says. "It can't be that bad if Becca's only in the infirmary. She'd be in the hospital if it were serious."

Tiffany agrees, reaches in her ever-present purse, and hands Tara a tissue.

Amanda rocks back in her chair and smiles. "Intense," she says with admiration. "That Becca chick is really intense."

I feel for the loose strip of metal at the edge of the table, bending it a little. With no warning it breaks off in my hand. Everyone is so busy worrying about Becca, they don't look at me. It's an accident, this thing snapping off into my hand, but I slip it in my pocket. Just in case.

The chimes ring; it's hard to leave.

"Remember that girl in my group I told you about," I say as soon as you close your door.

"Which one?" you say.

"Becca, the really skinny girl, the anorexic who's still throwing up?"

You nod.

"She . . . I . . ." Hot tears start to well up in my eyes; you become a blur of colors. "Something's wrong."

I look out the window, shading my eyes with my hands like the sun's too bright.

"What is it, Callie?" I steal a glance at you; your hands are pressed together in a praying gesture. "Tell me, please."

"We don't know what's wrong," I say, suddenly conscious that I've used the word *we*. I can't go on.

"She might have had another heart attack," I say finally, the words coming out in stop-start bursts.

You slide the tissue box across the carpet and leave it at my feet. "Can you tell me why you're so upset?"

"No." I feel foggy again, lost. "I really can't."

You lean back. "Would you feel better if I tell you what I know?"

I nod, vaguely startled and yet not surprised somehow

that you would know what's going on with the girls in my group.

"It wasn't a heart attack," you say.

I sit forward and wait for you to tell me more.

"The doctor said she did have an irregular heartbeat last night," you say. "And some palpitations."

"She didn't have a heart attack?" I need to be sure.

"No. They think she was probably just dehydrated."

"From throwing up?"

"That's a good possibility."

I wad up a tissue, throw it in the trash can, and grab another one. "So she's going to be OK?"

You blow out a long steady stream of air. "I can't say. She will be, if she begins taking responsibility for her health, for her recovery here. If she doesn't . . ." Your voice trails off.

"Debbie was really upset," I say.

"Debbie?"

"The girl who takes care of her."

"How could you tell?"

"She was eating pancakes," I say. "A lot of pancakes." I picture Debbie at the breakfast table, shoveling food into her mouth. And it dawns on me that seeing her eat like that might have grossed me out before—or annoyed me, or maybe even secretly pleased me. Now it just makes me sad.

"How do you feel?"

"Me? I don't know."

You don't seem completely satisfied with this answer.

"Tara. She was upset too." I want to talk about Debbie,

about Tara, about everybody else. "The new girl," I say. "She's weird."

You cock your head slightly.

"It was like she was happy it happened."

"Callie," you say. "What about *you*? How do *you* feel about what Becca did?"

Your eyes flick toward the clock, making a quick check. Without really thinking, I pat the outside of my pocket, feeling for the metal strip, telling myself it's there if I need it.

How do I feel? I feel like cutting. I don't know why. And I don't tell you.

Everyone's already there when I get to Group; the only chairs left are Becca's old seat and the one next to Debbie. Debbie's eyes are bloodshot, her eyelids painted with blue eye shadow, and her face is powdery white. She's obviously been crying. I slide into the chair next to her.

Claire starts off by saying that it looks like Becca's going to be OK, but that she'll have to be in the infirmary for a while.

"She didn't have a heart attack?" says Tara.

"Is she coming back?" says Sydney.

"Can I have her room?" says Tiffany.

Claire takes off her glasses and rubs the bridge of her nose. "Becca hasn't been eating; she was hiding her food, then throwing it away," she says. She holds her glasses up to the light, rubs out a smudge with a tissue. "She's also been throwing up what little she did eat."

"Now," she says, putting her glasses back on, "what we

need to talk about in this group are your feelings about Becca's actions."

Tiffany chews on her nails. Debbie chews her gum. I chew my lip. Then the room is quiet—so quiet we can hear the muffled sound of voices from the group next door.

"No volunteers?" Claire says at last. "OK. We'll go around the circle."

My heart hammers; we've never done this before. What will happen when it's my turn?

"Tiffany, why don't you go first?" Claire says.

I breathe out; Tiffany's four seats away from me.

Tiffany rolls her eyes, adjusts her purse strap. "It pisses me off," she says. "I don't know why, it just does." She turns to Tara.

Tara shrugs. Then she starts crying. She throws her hands up and turns toward Amanda. My heart beats double time; two more people and it'll be my turn.

"I didn't know her that well," Amanda says. "I mean I *don't* know her that well. It's not like she's dead or anything." She flashes a cocky smile around the circle.

"But how did you feel about it?" Claire says.

"Feel? Oh, I think it raised some issues for me. Fear of abandonment, self-loathing, repressed hostility, that sort of thing. Is that what you're looking for?"

Claire purses her lips; her gaze travels to Sydney. "Sydney, how about you?"

Sydney's next to me, but I can hardly hear her, my heart is pounding so hard.

98

"It bugged me." Sydney's voice cracks. She clears her throat. "It bugged me that she's, you know, doing that to herself. How could she do that to herself?" She starts crying, then turns to me.

I survey the circle. Tara gives me a teary smile from under the brim of her baseball cap. Amanda eyes me suspiciously. I pick at a hangnail.

Then Debbie leans over. "You don't have to say anything, Callie." She looks around the group. "Right, everyone?"

"Why can't you leave people alone?" says Tiffany. "Why can't you let *her* decide if she wants to talk? You're so worried about her. About trying to make sure she doesn't have to talk. I think *you're* the one who doesn't want to talk about it."

Debbie ignores her, turns to Claire. "She doesn't have to talk if she doesn't want to, does she?"

Claire sighs. "That's up to Callie," she says. "Callie, are you ready to talk today?"

"C'mon, S.T.," Sydney whispers.

I pull at the hangnail. Words take shape in my brain, a few, then a flood; then they're gone. I shake my head, a little at first, then harder, as I watch my hair swing from side to side.

"OK," says Claire. "Debbie?"

Debbie's arm brushes mine as she shifts in her chair.

There's silence, then the sound of more talking next door, then more silence.

"Scared."

I have to look out of the corner of my eye to make sure it's Debbie talking.

"Debbie," says Claire. "What is it you're afraid of?"

Debbie wrings her shirt in her hands. I don't move. "You're all going to be mad at me."

"Why do you think that?" says Claire.

Debbie shrugs. Her arm brushes mine again; it's soft and pillowy. I relax my grip a little.

"Debbie," Claire says in a gentle voice. "Can you look at me a minute?" We all look at her. "Why would we be angry with you?"

Debbie twists her shirt into a knot. "I should've tried to stop her."

People shift in their seats. Someone across the room coughs. Then nothing.

Tara raises her hand finally. "You couldn't have known what she was doing."

"I should have." Debbie looks around the group. "I know that's what you all think. I know you all hate me. You hate me for not taking care of Becca. I know it."

No one says anything.

Debbie plows her fists into her thighs. "It's not fair. I try to do what people want. At home, I do all the things no one else wants to do. I sort the recyclables, I clean the litter box, I do the wash . . ."

There's a long silence.

"Why?" says Sydney. Her voice is soft, curious.

Debbie shrugs.

"Why do you do things people don't even ask you to?"

Debbie shakes her head. "I don't know." She sounds exhausted. "I really don't." She sighs a long, tired sigh; when she's finished the room is quiet again. She sinks back into her chair, her arm resting against mine. I don't move away.

"It's not your fault."

The words come out of my mouth. I aim them at my lap. But they're for Debbie. From me.

I can hear people squirming in their chairs. Then the room is quiet again. I peer out from under my hair and take in the circle of feet. Everyone is wearing sneakers, except Amanda, who has on combat boots.

Debbie turns to look at me. "What did you say?" she whispers.

"It's not your fault," I say. "About Becca."

I keep my eyes on Amanda's boots; her legs are crossed and she's swinging her foot up and down.

"It's mine."

Amanda stops swinging her foot.

"I . . ." My voice gives out. I clear my throat. "I saw her . . . One time I saw her put her brownie in a napkin. And in the bathroom, I knew she was throwing up."

I lean back in my chair, feeling trembly and very, very tired. The silence is long and loud with things people aren't saying. I can't stand to look up and see their faces. To see how angry they are.

Footsteps echo in the hallway. They get louder and louder, then faint, then fainter, then they trail away.

"Hey, S.T.," Sydney says finally.

I don't budge.

101

She nudges me with her elbow. "You want to know something?"

I still can't look up. But I nod.

"It's not your fault either." She says this like it's no big deal. Like it's nothing.

But it's everything.

Group is over then and people are standing, gathering up their books, heading to their appointments. I keep my head down, grip the edge of my chair, and hold on like my life depends on it. I don't know what just happened in here, but I can't leave.

"S.T.?" It's Sydney's voice. "You coming?"

She's standing in front of me. Debbie's there, too. And Tara. And Claire. A semicircle of feet.

A weird strangling sound starts in my chest, then comes out my mouth. I'm crying—sobbing, actually, and gulping for air. I wipe my eyes; the feet are still there. But the crying won't stop. I'm shaking and trying not to shake, but it's no good. I can't stop. Claire says something about going to get help.

Finally a pair of white shoes pushes through the semicircle. Ruby's there, rubbing my back, saying, "There, there, baby. It's all right. It's going to be all right."

Then you're standing there, in your little fabric shoes, saying the same thing, that it's all right now.

You shut your door; I notice that it's getting dark outside and wonder if you'd be home walking your dog or making your dinner right now if I hadn't freaked out.

102

"Can you tell me what upset you so much in Group?"

I shrug. "Debbie." It's all I can say.

"How did Debbie upset you?"

"No." I blow my nose. "Debbie didn't do anything. I . . . she . . ." I rip the tissue in two and start again. "She thought it was her fault. About Becca."

I don't dare to look at you.

"I thought it was my fault," I whisper.

I glance at you, then away. You look worried.

"I think everything's my fault."

"What else is your fault?"

"I don't know. Everything. Sam."

"Sam?"

"Its my fault he's sick. Which means it's my fault my mom's not the same anymore and my fault my dad's not around. It's all my fault."

"Callie." Your voice is gentle. "How can all those things be your fault?"

"I don't know. They just are."

"How is it your fault that Sam is sick?"

"I made him cry? I got him upset?" I've always taken this for granted; as I say it out loud, though, it sounds stupid.

"Callie, I'm a doctor," you say. "If I tell you that a person doesn't get asthma from crying, from being upset, will you believe me?"

I shrug.

"Asthma is a kind of allergic reaction. People can develop it when they come in contact with certain substances, like

103

pollen or dust. Sometimes a viral infection can trigger an attack. But you can't give asthma to someone. The allergic response is already in their system."

The fog is clouding my mind again. What you're saying sounds like something from biology class; it doesn't have anything to do with me or Sam or my mom being scared all the time and my dad being gone all the time. I look for the rabbit on the ceiling but can't quite find him.

"Has anyone told you all these things are your fault?" you interrupt.

"No one has to. I just know."

"Does anyone punish you for these things?"

I shake my head.

"No one?"

I look up at you. You still look concerned.

"What about you? Aren't you punishing yourself? By hurting yourself?"

I don't understand. "No."

"Then why do you think you cut yourself?"

"I don't know." I tear the tissue to shreds. "It just happens. I can't help it."

You furrow your brow.

"I know it's bad," I say. "I guess I do it because I'm . . . bad."

"How are you bad?"

"I don't know. I just feel like I'm this bad person."

"What have you done that's so bad?"

"I don't know." As soon as I say it, I know it's the truest thing I've ever said. "I really don't know."

You look pleased and say that's enough for one day.

Right before dinner there's always a crowd of people on the smoking porch. As I go past, Sydney taps on the glass door. I stop and watch as she gestures for me to come out. Before I can decide what to do, she grinds out her cigarette and comes in to get me.

"C'mon, S.T.," she says, grabbing my arm. "Come outside with us."

I pull my sleeve down over my thumb and follow, trying to match her big strides as her ponytail bobs up and down in front of me.

"Guess I can't call you S.T. anymore." She waits at the door for me to catch up. "Now that you're talking."

"It's OK," I say. "You can still call me that."

There's a blast of cold, smoky air as Sydney opens the door. I step onto the porch, take in the curious looks of the other girls, and jam my hands into my pockets.

"Want one?" Sydney waves a pack of cigarettes in front of me. I shake my head and watch the careful way she lights up, cupping her hand around the match to keep it from blowing out. "My favorite addiction," she says, blowing out a fat white smoke ring.

Tiffany wanders over. "Does anybody else think it's weird that we're allowed to smoke here?" she says.

Sydney admires her smoke ring as it floats away. "Yeah," she says. "No barfing, no bingeing, no inhaling fumes from the art supplies. But smoking's OK."

The other girls laugh and I feel the corners of my mouth turn up. I lift my sleeve to my mouth, but the smile stays as they make jokes about the rules, about the food, about Group. It's cold outside and I wonder why no one ever wears a coat at Sick Minds. Mostly, though, I test out what it feels like to smile again.

I'm so tired that night that I fall asleep in my clothes. I'm sitting up in bed reading a story for English and the next thing I know Ruby's leaning over me, telling me it's almost lights-out.

"You want to put this on?" She's holding one of my night-gowns.

Then she's gone, her shoes squeaking down the hall. The room is dark; Sydney's on her back, sleeping. I get up slowly, then make my way down to the bathroom.

Rochelle's in her chair and Amanda's standing at the sink, although I hardly recognize her. She's washed off all her makeup—her pencil-arched brows, her black eyeliner, her red lipstick—and she looks very young. She's studying her face in the mirror, so she doesn't notice me right away. When she does, she scowls.

I find a corner, turn my back, and begin the process of getting undressed for the shower without letting her see me.

First I unhook my bra, tug the straps down, and pull it off from under my shirt. Then I drape the towel over my shoulders and take off my shirt, quickly pulling the towel around me, toga-style, as my shirt falls to the floor. Next I step out of my jeans, holding the towel in place with one hand and tugging my pants off with the other. I'm balanced on one foot, kicking off my pants leg, when something metal hits the tile floor with a tiny plink.

The metal strip from the dining room table: I'd forgotten it was still in my pocket. Instinctively I slide my foot across the tile, covering the piece of metal.

Rochelle's head bobs up, but she looks in the wrong direction, over at the toilet stalls. But Amanda turns quickly toward me. She takes in my awkward position, the towel gripped to my chest, one foot half stuck inside my pants leg, the other stretched out uncomfortably far away, across the floor. Then she nods slowly, approvingly.

"Rochelle," she calls out, still looking at me. "Is there anyone down at the desk? I need something."

I'm too startled to move. Is she going to tell on me, get me in trouble?

Rochelle's gotten up; she's banging the toilet stall doors open one by one, checking to make sure no one's in there. When the last stall turns up empty, she gives Amanda an annoyed look. "What do you need this time of night?"

Amanda smiles at me, then turns to face Rochelle. "A tampon."

I don't understand. Then I do. Amanda's sending Rochelle off on a fake errand so I can pick up the metal strip and hide it.

Rochelle sighs. "You two aren't food-disorder girls, right? You're not gonna throw up if I leave for a minute?"

We nod, almost in unison.

"OK," she says. "I'm trusting you. No funny business."

We nod.

Rochelle leaves. Amanda is next to me all of a sudden. I slide my foot back and the metal strip is lying there on the floor between us.

"Where'd you get it?" she says.

"The dining room table. It broke off."

"Gutsy," she says. "Real gutsy."

She seems so delighted at the sight of the strip, I think maybe she's going to take it. I picture myself grabbing it and just dropping it in the trash can right in front of her. Instead I pick it up, close my fingers around it, and head for the shower before Rochelle comes back. The hairs on my neck tingle, as if Amanda might grab me at any minute and pry the metal strip out of my hand. But she doesn't.

I turn the water on high and listen while Amanda thanks Rochelle for the tampon. A toilet stall door opens, closes, then opens again, and I hear Amanda call out good night in a sing-song voice. Slowly I take off my towel, wrap the metal strip in it, and get in the shower. When it's time to go back to my room, I put the piece of metal back in my pants, folding

108

them carefully so it doesn't fall out. I'll figure out what to do with it later.

I feel suddenly shy when I sit down across from you in your office today. Something happened between us yesterday, and I don't quite know how to come back from it. You smile and a good warm feeling comes over me. I settle into the cushions of the couch, deciding that I'll work hard today, try to come up with the right answers to your questions.

"How are you?" you say.

"Fine." This is true, but it sounds inadequate. I give you a practice smile. You smile back.

"Callie," you say, folding your hands around your knees. "What you did yesterday—speaking out in Group—that was a big step."

"It was?" I want to hear more.

"It took a lot of courage."

My checks get warm, an uncomfortable and at the same time not uncomfortable feeling.

"How did it feel to speak in front of the other girls?"

"OK." I try to come up with a better answer. "A little scary, I guess."

"What were you afraid of?"

"That people would get mad at me."

"Hmmm." You nod. "Who did you think would be angry?"

"I don't know," I say. "Everybody?"

"Everybody?"

I shrug. The foggy feeling settles over me. I want to give you a right answer, but I don't have one.

"Let me ask you this: do people get angry with you a lot?"

"Not really."

You wait.

"My mom cries a lot but she doesn't yell or anything," I say.

"And your father . . ."

I chew on a hangnail. "He doesn't get too worked up," I say finally.

A car tire spins on the ice outside.

"I've noticed that you don't talk about your father much."

My leg muscles tighten, I feel ready to run. I cross and recross my legs, trying hard to just stay in my seat. "So?" I say.

"What can you tell me about him?" you say.

"Don't you have stuff in your file?" I say after a while.

"I don't really know much about him. I met with your mother on visiting day, but your dad wasn't here."

"He has to work." I remember scanning the parking lot for him, watching somebody's dad come up the sidewalk, banging on the window, and realizing it wasn't him.

You tap your file. "He's a computer salesman, is that right?"

Your file makes it sound like he works at RadioShack; for some reason, this makes me mad. "He sells computers to companies. He takes people out to dinner and stuff to get them to buy whole, big computer systems."

You don't seem to understand.

"He has to travel."

You still don't say anything.

"Well, he used to. Travel, I mean. Since Sam got sick, he changed jobs. Now he just sells to companies nearby." I don't tell you about how it seems like all the companies nearby already have computers, that for a while he took people out hoping they'd become customers and that now he mostly just goes out. "He has to work a lot."

"Is that why he wasn't here for visiting day?"

A muscle in my leg is twitching, my heart is hammering against my ribs. All I want to do is jump off the couch and run. I cross my legs again, winding one around the other to keep them still. "I don't feel like talking about this anymore."

I draw my mouth into a straight line and bite my lip. Somehow some of the good warm feeling from yesterday is gone.

"Callie?"

I chew on my lip, a little harder now.

"Callie, you're biting your lip."

I meet your eyes for a second, then look out the window at the bare branch of the tree.

"Do you know the expression 'bite your lip'?"

"I guess so."

"Tell me what you think it means."

"Y'know," I say, my eyes locked on the branch. "To shut up. To not say something."

"To not say something." You recite my words.

I go back to biting my lip.

Your dead-cow chair groans as you lean forward. "Callie, I feel like there's something you're not saying."

Now everything good from yesterday is gone.

We're in the middle of Group and Tiffany is telling us about some guy she had sex with behind the dumpster at her school. She's saying something about how it's his fault she's at Sick Minds, because he told his friends, who told some of her friends, who told the health teacher, who Tiffany then had to beat up.

The door opens. We all turn to see who it is. It's Becca. Becca being pushed in a wheelchair by an actual nurse, someone in a white uniform.

Tiffany stops in mid-sentence.

Claire nods. "Welcome back, Becca," she says.

Becca wiggles her fingers hello. "Hi, everybody," she says.

No one says anything.

"Becca's going to continue working with our group," Claire says carefully. "And eventually we hope she'll be back with us full time, but for the time being she's staying on another ward."

We all know what this means: Humdinger.

Becca giggles; everyone else squirms. The nurse wheels Becca's chair into a space next to Amanda. Amanda nudges her chair aside a little, then folds her arms across her chest and looks sideways at Becca. The nurse locks the brakes on the wheelchair and leaves.

Dead quiet.

"You look good," someone says finally. It's Sydney. Her voice is shaky, her eyes dart nervously around the circle.

Becca makes a gagging gesture, sticking her tongue out and pointing a finger down her throat. "They tube-fed me." She grins sheepishly.

There's another long silence.

"You don't think I look fat?" Becca giggles again.

Debbie jumps out of her chair and heads for the door.

"No, Debbie," says Claire. "You need to stay here."

Debbie turns around. Her jaw is clenched; a vein is pulsing in her neck.

Claire is pointing to Debbie's empty chair. Debbie harrumphs across the room and flops into her seat.

No one moves.

Becca flips her hair over her shoulder. "So, what?" she says. "Are you guys mad at me or something?"

Sydney coughs. Then nothing.

"Yes," comes a tiny voice from across the circle. It's Tara. She's looking out at Becca from under her baseball cap.

Becca grins, like she can't believe it, like it's a big joke. "Why?" she says. "I'm OK. See?" She clamps her teeth together and smiles hard.

No one says anything.

"Besides, I don't see what the big deal is," Becca says. She looks at Claire, then back at the group. "It's not like I did anything to you guys."

Debbie snorts.

"Yes," says Tara. "Yes, you did." She looks down at her lap, cracks her knuckles. "What you did affected all of us. Me. Debbie. Callie. All of us."

Us. This is the first time I've been included in *us.* My cheeks flush.

Becca's gaze travels around the circle; she looks hopeful and doubtful at the same time.

"We . . ." Tara can't finish.

"We were scared," says Sydney, all in a rush. "We . . . you know, we want you to get better. That's why we're all here, isn't it? To get better?"

I check to see how people are responding to this question. Tara nods. Debbie nods. Tiffany shrugs. Amanda checks her watch.

Becca looks stunned.

Claire finally says something. "Becca? How are you doing?"

Becca doesn't answer.

"You look upset."

Becca nods, then says to Claire, "Is it OK if I go back to the infirmary for a while?"

Claire says that's fine, that maybe this is a lot to take in on her first day back; then she goes to the door and signals an attendant. Marie comes, releases the brake on Becca's chair, and wheels her away.

When Becca's gone, we all sit there looking at Debbie. Mascara is running down her cheeks and a muscle is working in her jaw, but she's staring off into space.

"You OK?" says Sydney at last.

Debbie nods vacantly.

People look around, not sure what to do.

"Are you sure?" says Tara.

"Yeah," Debbie says, finally breaking off her stare. "Yeah," she says. "I'm fine."

Then she turns to me.

"What about *you*?" she says, wiping her face with the back of her hand. "Are you OK?"

I can feel heads turning around the circle to look at me. "Sure," I say. "Yeah."

Debbie smiles, then claps a hand over her mouth. "I did it again!" she says. "Taking care of everybody else. What do you call it, Amanda?"

Amanda's face is a mixture of surprise and mischief. "Co-dependent," she says. "You're being co-dependent again."

Debbie laughs. It's a nervous laugh, but everyone laughs, too, out of relief. All of us.

Now that I've been upgraded to a Level Two, I can escort myself places. Tonight I'm on my way to the game room, even though I don't really feel like playing Connect Four, and even though everyone else is in the dayroom. I really feel like watching TV because I haven't seen a single show since I got here, but I'm not sure I can just walk in and sit down with everybody after all this time. I walk past the door and notice Tara's baseball cap turning as I go by.

"Callie?" I turn around and see her running down the

hall behind me. She scuffs along in her slippers, then slides to a stop when she gets to me, like one of Sam's hockey players.

"Hey!" She's panting. The thought crosses my mind that Tara could have a heart attack if she doesn't get better. I stop and wait for her to catch her breath.

"Whew!" She smiles. "We were wondering if you wanted to watch TV." She tips her head toward the dayroom. "You know, with the group. Unless you don't want to. It's OK if you want to be alone."

She's still breathing hard.

"Sure," I say, looking at her hopeful, embarrassed face. "Sure."

Sydney and Debbie are on the couch. Tiffany's on the floor, flipping through a magazine and watching TV at the same time. Sydney looks up when I come in, slides down the couch, and pats the seat next to her. "S.T.," she says. "Sit here."

The couch is a big bumpy overstuffed thing and when I sit back my feet don't touch the floor. Tara sits down next to me and I notice that her feet don't touch, either. They're watching *Jeopardy*; it's time for the daily double. A contestant named Tim has chosen Silent Film Stars for $500. The host asks the big question: "This actress, dubbed America's Sweetheart, starred in the original film version of *Heidi*."

"C'mon, Tim," Sydney chants.

"Shirley Temple?" suggests Debbie.

"No," says Tiffany. "It's a silent film star."

I know this one. I know the answer. I know it from watching TV with Sam on Saturday afternoons when our mom is resting. "Mary Pickford," I whisper. Then louder, "Mary Pickford."

Tim hits his buzzer. "Who was Mary Pickford?"

The daily double alarm goes off. Tim jumps up and down. Sydney thumps me on the back. "Way to go, S.T.! You win the daily double!"

The next morning at breakfast, Tiffany announces flatly that she's going home. "The insurance ran out," she says, pushing her scrambled eggs around on her plate. "They thought I could stay for a couple of months, but now they say they'll pay for only a month—which is over today."

"You lucky dog," says Amanda.

Tiffany grunts.

"Aren't you happy?" says Tara.

Tiffany puts salt on her eggs, pushes them around some more, then sets her fork down. "No."

"Why not? I thought you hated it here."

Tiffany shakes her head. "You think *this* place is crazy, you should try living with my family."

A couple of people nod. No one seems able to eat.

"What will you do?" says Sydney after a while. "You know, to get better?"

"They're sending me to some outpatient thing. Some group that meets after school every day." Tiffany waves her hand like she's brushing away a fly.

"Why can't you go to school and come to Group here in the afternoon?" says Sydney.

"It's too far, I guess," Tiffany says glumly. Then, quietly, "It won't be the same."

The chimes ring; no one moves. Then Claire comes over and tells us our group doesn't have to go straight to our usual appointments; we're allowed to walk Tiffany to the front door.

We all stand around in a circle in the reception room, waiting for Tiffany's cab and not talking about her leaving—all of us except Amanda, who didn't come out of her room when it was time to walk to the front door. Tiffany's belongings hardly fill a plastic bag and she looks small somehow, fingering the latch of her purse and pretending like she could care less about leaving.

Finally a cab pulls up and blows the horn. Sydney gives Tiffany a hug. Tara says she'll write. Debbie tells Tiffany she'll actually miss her. "You never let me get away with . . . you know, crap." It's a big deal for Debbie to say *crap* and I think maybe she's going to laugh, but her eyes are brimming with wetness.

Tiffany punches me in the arm lightly and tells me I have to keep talking in Group. I nod. Then I realize that nodding isn't talking. "OK," I say. I want to say "I promise," but my throat closes up on me.

Just when everyone, including Tiffany, looks like they're going to start crying, Sydney says, "Hey, now that you're leaving . . . why don't you tell us why you always carry that darn purse?"

Tiffany fiddles with the latch. "You promise you won't tell?"

We promise.

She opens the purse and pulls out a ratty piece of pink fabric. "My old baby blanket." She grins and shrugs and then turns to go.

When the automatic doors slide apart, a warm, moist riffle of air floats in, lifting the hair around my face. The snow has melted; tiny green buds are forming on the tips on the trees. It dawns on me that soon it will be spring. Then summer. Kids will be riding their bikes on the sidewalk, dads will be rolling out barbecue grills, moms will be making pitchers of lemonade.

The doors slide shut and it's winter again inside Sick Minds.

An ache fills my chest. I want something, but I can't put a name to it.

Debbie, Sydney, Tara, and I shuffle back to the dorm, not saying anything. When we get to the attendants' desk, we drift apart; no one's in a hurry to go to their appointments, especially me, since I have Study Hall. I see Ruby putting on her coat, going off duty.

"What day is it in the real world, Ruby?" I ask, when the other girls are gone.

"The real world? What do you mean, child?"

"Out there." I point to the window. "What day is it?"

"Wednesday."

"No, I mean the date. What's the date?"

She looks over at the chalkboard. Tiffany's name has already been erased. Sydney and Tara have been upgraded to Level Threes, along with Debbie. Next to Becca's name it simply says "H Wing." Our group is down to five: Sydney, Tara, and Debbie, who are going to graduate soon, and Amanda and me.

"March 27," Ruby says.

She says it's time for her to go home and get some sleep. She says they're doing construction in her neighborhood, and she sure hopes they're finished with the jackhammer. She appraises me, then smiles. She says not to worry and slips me a butterscotch candy. But the wanting feeling still doesn't go away.

Later, after Study Hall, I escort myself to your office. The lights in the waiting area are off and the UFOs outside all the shrink offices are quiet. I sit down in my usual chair outside your door and wait. I check my watch. If this were a dentist's office, there'd be old *National Geographic*s to look at; here, there are only tissue boxes and more tissue boxes.

I check my watch again.

You're late. Fifteen minutes late.

I count the tissue boxes and the UFOs. I do the math; there are 1.5 tissue boxes per UFO. I check my watch again and know that you're not coming. That something's wrong.

I must have made a mistake. The chalkboard probably says my appointment was changed. That happens sometimes. I decide to wait until you're twenty minutes late; then I'll check the chalkboard.

Then it dawns on me: Wednesday is your day off. I remember you saying *See you Thursday*, last time. You didn't say *See you tomorrow*. You said *See you Thursday*. I feel annoyed for some reason, then scared. Thursday is a long time away. What will I do till then?

I decide to go to Study Hall and figure out how many hours till tomorrow. How many hours, then how many minutes, then how many seconds. That will at least help pass the time.

Study Hall's closed, too. My only other choice is the dayroom. When I walk in, the TV's on, but no one's watching it; then I see Amanda lying down on the couch. She notices me before I can sneak out.

"So," she says, "you were onto Becca's scam?"

I don't know how to answer. Her voice is cajoling, full of encouragement; I think I'm supposed to say yes, but somehow I don't. I shrug.

"Cool," she says, sitting up. "Very cool."

I sit down on a chair far from her and act very interested in the show on TV, a rerun of *Family Ties*. Alex is trying to keep his mom from opening the closet.

"So, S.T.," Amanda says. "What do you use?"

I don't understand.

She pulls up her sleeve and points to a line of purplish bumps on the inside of her arm; she twists her hand so I can see that the bumps go all the way around her wrist, like a bracelet. "You know, scissors? Glass? Wire?"

I try to concentrate on the TV. The *Family Ties* mom turns her back and the person hiding in the closet opens the door; Alex slams it shut, looking innocent. I can't exactly follow it with Amanda bugging me.

"I knew a girl who used her father's credit card. Nice touch. Little hidden psychological message in that, don't you think?"

I don't say anything.

"My personal favorite?" Amanda maneuvers herself so she's blocking my view of the TV. "A safety pin and hairspray. Rubbing alcohol's good, too. But hairspray's the best. It makes your scars puff up."

She lies down again. "By the way," she says, "I found this staple. Underneath one of the chairs in the study lounge. It works really well."

I remember the look on her face in Study Hall the day I saw her rubbing her arm on the seat of the chair while she pretended to be asleep.

"Third row, last chair," she says. "Just thought you might want to know. In case they find your metal thing."

On Thursday I don't wait for you to ask me where I want to start. While you're still closing your door, I ask if you want to see my scars.

Your face is neutral. "Do you want to show me?" you say.

I nod. I pinch my sleeve between my thumb and index finger, but instead of pulling it up, I pull it down. Until it covers my wrist. Until it covers my hand. Until my whole arm is hidden inside my sleeve.

"I use my mom's Exacto knife." I stare at my shirtsleeve. "Or her embroidery scissors. Once I used the paper towel dispenser in the guest bathroom here." I feel the corners of my mouth turn up; I'm not happy, but somehow I have to fight the urge to smile.

I check for your reaction. You're expecting something, I can tell. Your normal, calm face shows a hint of waiting. Waiting, and something else, something like hope.

I roll my sleeve between my thumb and index finger, then deliberately, with a kind of reverence, I pull my sleeve back, all the way up to the elbow, and extend my arm to you.

You're not disgusted or frightened or any of the hundred wrong things you could be; you look like yourself, serious, curious, and maybe, maybe, just a little bit proud of me.

I look at my arm. It's crisscrossed with pink lines, lines that strike me as delicate and faint, lines I remember making.

I gently pull my sleeve back down and decide it would be good to make some kind of joke right about now.

"Guess I'll never wear a strapless ball gown," I say.

You look perplexed.

"Debbie, you know Debbie from my group, she's always drawing fancy ball gowns. I'll have to ask her to design one for me—one that has long sleeves." I laugh. You don't.

"What makes you think you'll never wear a strapless ball gown?"

I shrug. I never planned on wearing fancy clothes, but for some dumb reason, now I really want to. In fact I want to so badly, I feel like crying. "I don't know."

"You might wear a ball gown someday." You say this quite surely.

"I might?"

You nod. "I have every reason to believe you'll do all the things every other girl does, all the things you want to do."

I'm still stuck on the stupid ball gown that I never cared about until now. "With these arms?" I thrust my arms out, keeping my sleeves wrapped around my thumbs.

"Those scars will fade. It looks like some have already faded."

I consider this.

"There are treatments, too, medical treatments that can help get rid of scars."

I must look dubious because you go on.

"I knew a little girl who was in a terrible car accident. A beautiful little girl whose face was absolutely covered with cuts; she had nearly a hundred stitches in her face."

I wince. I feel so sad, so sorry for this little girl, I want you to stop. But I need to hear more.

"She's a model now," you say. "She's a very successful, very beautiful model. She had plastic surgery to get rid of her scars. You would never know what happened to her when she was younger."

I like and don't like this story; but I don't know why.

A bird outside your window trills. Another bird, far off, answers.

"I may not want to get rid of my scars," I say finally.

You nod.

"They tell a story," I say.

"Yes," you say, "they do."

It must be the end of our time because you're standing up. I wait for you to say *Good work, see you tomorrow.* But you just stand there with your hand on the doorknob. I get to my feet and look at the clock. Our time was up a few minutes ago. I tug at the hem of my shirt.

"Callie," you say. "Is there something else you want to say?"

I shake my head. But I don't move.

"You seem to be waiting. Can you tell me what you're waiting for?"

I shake my head again. Then I nod.

You let go of the doorknob.

I reach into my pocket and pull out the metal strip. "It's from the cafeteria," I say.

You don't seem to understand. I hold it out toward you.

"You're giving this to me?"

I keep my eyes on the stain on the carpet and nod.

"Can you tell me why?"

"Not really." I roll my feet onto the sides of my sneakers. "So I don't . . . you know . . ." I know I have to say more. "So I don't use it."

I look up from the carpet to check your reaction. You're tapping your lip with your finger.

"I'm glad," you say finally. "I'm very happy that you don't want to use this to hurt yourself."

My arm is getting tired; the metal strip feels very, very heavy. Finally, when you reach out and take it, it slips from my fingers, weightless. You place it on the corner of your desk.

"I'll keep it here until you're ready to decide what you want to do with it."

I don't understand. "I get it back?" I look over at the small, dull square of metal sitting on the edge of your desk, so close I could just reach out and slip it back in my pocket.

"Callie." Your voice is a little sad. "There are all kinds of things in the world you could use to hurt yourself. All kinds of things you could turn into weapons. Even if you wanted to give them all to me, it wouldn't be possible. You know that, don't you?"

I do know that, I guess. I nod.

"I can't keep you safe," you say. "Only you can."

That night we see Becca in the dining room with her new group from Humdinger. Maybe I've been here too long—they don't look that bad to me.

Becca walks past our table carrying a glass of water; behind her, another girl, who looks normal except for the twitchy smile on her face, is carrying two trays. They get to their table and the girl sets one of the trays down in

126

front of Becca, pulls out a chair for her, then hands her a napkin.

Debbie is staring; then she shades her eyes, still watching Becca and her new friend. Finally she turns to Amanda. "Guess Becca's found somebody new to be co-dependent."

We go back to our dinners, trying not to look at Becca anymore. The pasta tonight is especially bland. I consider going to the salad bar. I check first to see if the Ghost is there, waltzing. She's not.

"Where's the Ghost?" I ask Sydney.

"Home," she says. "She went home."

Tara and Sydney complain about the food, but I don't really pay attention. I'm thinking about how people leave here: Ruth, Tiffany, the Ghost. Some leave on schedule, some leave without warning. But everyone leaves eventually.

Tara's asked me a question. I can tell because everyone is looking at me.

"Huh?"

"Is it OK with you if we let Debbie have the remote tonight?"

"Sure," I say. "Absolutely." It's a simple question, the kind of thing the group used to vote on all the time, but this time, I'm included.

Debbie flips through the channels so fast it's hard to tell which shows she's rejecting. She stops briefly at the Food Channel, where a woman in an apron is making apple brown betty in what looks like a real kitchen.

"No," Debbie says, pushing the button on the remote. "Watching someone make dessert is not a good idea."

She flips through a few more stations, then stops at a show where all you can see is the front door of a house. A scratchy voice comes on: "What is the nature of your emergency?" A subtitle repeating these words scrolls by at the bottom of the screen. A child's voice, barely audible, comes next: "My mommy's on the floor." The child starts crying. The subtitle says: "(Child crying.)"

"*Rescue 911!*" Sydney shouts. "I love this show."

Debbie is transfixed, watching the screen. "Me too." She doesn't even look over at Sydney.

"Oh, wow," says Tara. "I used to watch this all the time."

"Me too," I say, aware that I sound surprised.

Sydney glances at me. "S.T.," she says in the weary old voice Sam used when he was trying to get me to understand lateral thinking. "*Everyone* loves this show."

"I don't think I have anything to talk about today," I say to you.

You nod.

"I mean, things are going really well," I say.

You smile.

"I talk in Group, at dinner, I'm getting along with the other girls."

"Good," you say.

"~~We all~~ watched TV together last night."

You seem to be waiting for more.

128

"Oh," I say. "We watched that show I told you about. *Rescue 911.*"

Your expression doesn't change. I wonder if you've ever watched *Rescue 911.* I wonder, again, what your life is like outside Sick Minds, if you watch TV like other people.

"*Everyone* loves that show," I tell you.

You don't agree or disagree. I wonder if you think it's stupid to talk about a TV show in therapy.

"It's really good. But it's also like a home video. You know, the camera is shaky sometimes, like when they show the paramedics carrying the person to the ambulance."

You don't seem especially interested; I want you to understand about this show.

"They make the ambulance sound really loud on the show. Sam says you can't hear the siren in real life."

"Sam rode in an ambulance?"

"Yeah." Now you seem to be paying attention; I decide to tell you more. "Actually, I gave him CPR before they got there."

"Before the paramedics got there?"

"Before my parents got there." I stop a second, confused. We've entered new territory here, talking about Sam and the ambulance and the paramedics and my parents; I can't quite remember what I've told you before. I need to change the subject, quickly.

"You may have saved his life," you say plainly.

"Huh?" The idea crosses my mind idly that saying *Huh* is bad manners; I should have said *Pardon me.*

"You may have saved Sam's life." You say this so simply, it almost seems sensible.

"No, I didn't."

You lean forward. "Why do you say that?"

"I don't know. That only happens to kids on TV."

"Like the kids on *Rescue 911*?"

"Yeah, I guess."

"You gave your little brother CPR. You got help. Why isn't that like the kids on *Rescue 911*?"

"I don't know. It just isn't."

"Well," you say. I see a distinct glimmer of impatience in your eyes. "I disagree."

I'm having trouble taking all this in: this new, sort of annoyed look in your eyes and this odd new idea.

It makes sense, then it doesn't. It seems right—here in a shrink's office in a loony bin called Sea Pines where there's no sea and no pines—but it can't be right in the real world.

"Callie?"

I try to focus on you. You seem very far away.

"What are you thinking about right now? Will you tell me?"

I'm thinking about the other day when you told me how people get asthma, how you said they can get it from having an infection.

"Sam had an infection," I hear myself say.

You wait.

"He wasn't feeling good that day. The day he got so sick."

I can picture him, wiping his nose and rubbing his eyes. "A cold or something. When my mom called about it, the doctor said to keep an eye on him."

"The day Sam had his first asthma attack, he was already sick?"

I nod.

"And the doctor said to keep an eye on him?"

I wonder why you care about this so much. I nod once, slowly this time.

"But your parents went out."

"My mom had to go see Gram at the nursing home."

"And your father?"

I shrug.

"He was out?"

"Yes," then quickly, "No. Well, I guess. He had to. It's OK."

"Where did he go?"

I bite my lip. "Out."

"Callie, we're out of time for today, but I want you to think about something."

I glance at you, then away.

"Please," you say. "Please try to see that day from a slightly different perspective. Try to imagine it as if you were on the outside looking in. Try to think of yourself in that situation as someone else, just a girl, a thirteen-year-old girl on her own, alone, with a sick little boy."

I don't see what good this will do, and I don't plan to do

131

it, I plan to forget about everything and go watch TV with the other girls, but I agree.

"Good," you say. "Good work, Callie. Excellent."

No one's in the dayroom; the TV's broken. I wander around and end up in Study Hall. No one's in there either, except Cynthia, the attendant with the large multiple-choice workbook. She smiles, goes back to her work.

I take my old seat by the window and watch the dog behind the maintenance shed. He barks, trots to the end of his chain, barks, trots back down the dirt path to his doghouse. I wonder if he's the dog I always hear barking during Group.

It's cold in here studying. I wrap my arms around myself and wish Debbie were here with her sweater. I wish Debbie were here, and Sydney and Tara, even Amanda. I pull my shirt close to me and think about going back to my room for a sweatshirt. I can do that now that I'm a Level Two; I could just get up and leave. I think about it, think about walking past the chair where Debbie draws her ball gowns, past the chair where Tara was sleeping when I slipped her the note from Sydney, past Amanda's chair. Amanda's chair: the one with the staple underneath.

I breathe out with a little shuddery sound. Cynthia looks up.

"You cold?"

I nod.

"Look at you, you're shivering," she says. "Why don't you go get yourself a sweater?"

I don't move.

"You're a Two now, right? It's OK for you to be on your own."

I rise to my feet, but I don't go anywhere. I'm thinking about you, about what you said about me being a girl on my own, alone, with a sick boy.

"Go on," she says.

I wonder suddenly if you'll tell my mom what I said about my dad being out when Sam was sick. My mom'll get upset, then Sam'll get upset, they'll get sick. Sam could even die. He could be having an attack right now and I'm not there. What if Sam is having an attack right now and I'm not there?

"Go on," Cynthia says again, insistent. "You're always in here. It'll do you good to get out of this place."

I know what to do then. I know exactly what to do.

III

i get up and go down the hall. Past the attendants' desk, past Rochelle on her orange plastic chair. She puts her finger on the page of her magazine to mark the spot, looks up, goes back to her reading. I pass the dayroom, which is still empty, and our Group room, which is also empty. I go by Amanda's room, the phone booth, my room. Down the stairs to the laundry room, past the fire exit with the YOU ARE HERE sign. I stand in front of a door marked EXIT.

I push the handle and wait for it to hold fast. To refuse to budge. But it opens. Easily and noiselessly. There's a tiny metallic clink as the latch gives way, then a clank as the door falls shut behind me. Then silence. The only sound after that is the soft crunching of grass as my feet travel across the lawn.

I start running. The motion of running—the cycle of one foot appearing as the other disappears, the forward swing of one arm, then the other—comes back to me effortlessly. I feel good. I put more distance between me and the YOU ARE HERE door. Then I feel a hundred eyes on my back, so I stop and turn around. The large picture window in the Group room is dark. Next to it, there's a narrow box of cold purple light—the bathroom window, where the light is always on. After the bathroom comes a row of black squares, dorm windows where no one's home, then a square of yellow light, which I think is my room, where Sydney has probably just come back from Art Therapy and is sprawled out on her bed, listening to her headphones, before the chimes sound for dinner.

I turn and start running again; this time, it's hard to get going. I put on a burst of speed, lose my balance and stumble a little, then get back in my rhythm. The last open space between Sick Minds and the outside world is the maintenance shed. After that, woods.

The dog who lives next to the maintenance building is standing outside his house, poised, watching me. I wait for him to bark, to let everyone know I'm out here, but he doesn't. I can see his foggy puffs of breath in the cold twilight. But he doesn't move; he doesn't make a sound.

Getting through the woods beyond Sick Minds is easy, much easier than I would have thought. The trees are evenly spaced, with plenty of room between them, as if someone planted them in rows. I look up past their trunks; above is a canopy of boughs. They are pine trees after all. I want to laugh. I want to turn around and go tell Sydney that Sea Pines actually does have some pines. But I don't. I keep running.

There's no fence, no wall at the edge of the property; I make a note of this, too, thinking how funny it would be to tell the other girls about how there's nothing really keeping us inside this loony bin. But I keep running, until the next thing I know, I'm on the side of a road. I pass an old brick house, then a cluster of newer houses; I run through an intersection, then onto the shoulder that runs alongside a highway with stores and more stores on either side.

I don't know how long I've been running. I try to notice, then memorize, the things I pass, but as soon as I tell myself to remember that there was a Dairy Queen on the left, it's gone and I can't remember if it was on the right or the left and if it was a Dairy Queen or a Burger King.

As I put more distance behind me and I feel the white-out effect coming on, I try to hold one thing in my mind: my home address. I say it over and over and over, like the words to a magic spell. I repeat the house number, the road name, the town, the state, the zip code, the house number, the road name, the town, the state, the zip code.

After a while my mouth gets dry and my legs ache. It starts to get dark; drivers put on their headlights. My feet get heavy and clumsy; I weave a little, up on the paved white line at the side of the road, then back down on the shoulder. A horn blares from behind me; I trip, suddenly awake, gravel spraying under my feet before I catch my balance. Up ahead, on a pole, is a pay phone, I decide that the pay phone is my goal.

Suddenly I doubt I even have the energy to make it the thirty or so steps to go that far. My feet scrape along the road, my knees go up and then down, but the pay phone doesn't seem to get any closer. I stop and wonder how there can be so little difference between running and stopping. I pick up one foot and then the other, and force myself to walk the last few steps.

The receiver is icy cold in my hand. I stare at it a minute and remember then that I have no money. I hang up, then pick it up again. I know you're not supposed to dial 911 unless it's an emergency, but I can't remember what the other choices are. I study the face of the phone, its neat grid of square buttons. Tucked in at the bottom is one that says "0." I push it and wonder if I'll get a real person or a recording.

A real person, a woman who sounds like she's in a room with lots of other operators, says, "Operator. How may I assist you?" She seems to be in a big hurry. A truck rattles by, practically blowing me off my feet. "Operator," she repeats. She's already fed up with me, I can tell. I hang up.

I circle the telephone pole, wondering what I was supposed to say to her. Another truck goes by; the wind cuts through my shirt. I wrap my arms around myself and wait to feel warmer; I feel colder. I pick up the receiver, push the 0, and pray for a different operator to pick up.

"Operator. May I help you?" This one has a tired, nice-sounding voice.

"Yes. Yes, you can," I say. "Please."

There's nothing on the other end; I wonder if she's still there.

"I need to call my dad." I didn't know I was going to say this; it just comes out.

There's no sound for a minute, then she says, "You want to make that a collect call?"

"Yes. Yes, please," I say. I give her my dad's work number and listen to a quick succession of beeps, like the beginning of a tune I used to know. My dad answers with the name of the computer company he works for. I picture him smoothing out his tie and smiling his business smile.

"Daddy?" I say.

The nice, tired operator interrupts, politely telling my dad that he has a collect call from Callie. "Will you accept?"

"Yes, yes, of course," he says. I hear two voices at once, my dad saying "Callie?" and the operator thanking him for using her phone company. Then cars whiz by and I can't hear anything.

"Callie? Are you all right?"

I shiver. "Fine." I meant to say *I'm fine*, but only *Fine* made it out.

"Where are you?"

I look around. There's a carpet sign with big paper S-A-L-E letters in the window. "I don't know for sure." The carpet store could be anywhere. I could be right around the corner from our house or a million miles away. "I ran away."

"From Sea Pines?" I picture him covering his eyes with his hand, the way he does when he's watching his favorite football team lose on Saturday afternoon TV.

I nod. "Uh-huh."

"Can you tell me what's nearby?"

Across the highway is an official blue state crest that says ROUTE 22. Underneath is a small square sign that says EAST. Beyond it is a Dunkin' Donuts.

"Route 22," I say. "East, I guess. Across from a Dunkin' Donuts."

He makes a *tkk, tkk* sound, the same noise he makes when he's paying the bills. "Sayville," he says. "You must be at the Dunkin' Donuts in Sayville."

I feel a little better knowing he knows where I am, even if I don't.

"That's about fifteen minutes from here," he says. "Can you wait for me there? Can you find a place to wait? Go inside the Dunkin' Donuts, OK?" I can hear the squeak of his chair and I picture him standing up, pushing his chair away from the desk, and grabbing his keys. "I'll be there as soon as I can."

Cars whoosh by, so I'm not sure if he said good-bye.

I stand on the lip of the highway waiting for a break in the traffic so I can cross over to the Dunkin' Donuts. Cars stream down the highway in an endless flow in either direction. When it's clear on one side, it's busy on the other. Finally I cross halfway and stand on a strip of concrete in the middle of the road as the cars whiz past, practically sucking me up into their wake. After a while I make a dash for it.

The Dunkin' Donuts is warm and bright; two men in coveralls are the only customers. They seem to be together at the counter, but they're not talking to each other, just reading different parts of the same paper side by side. I take a seat down at the other end and study the plastic labels under the rows of doughnuts. There are chocolate-dipped, chocolate-frosted, cream-filled, custard-filled, jelly-filled. Too many choices. I sit there and concentrate on not shivering.

The swinging door to the kitchen opens and a waitress in a pink apron and hat comes out. She refills the men's coffee without even asking if they want more, then comes and stands in front of me. Her plastic name tag says she's Peggy. "What'll it be?" she says.

What will what be? I wonder.

She looks me over. "You wanna order?" she says.

"Oh," I say. "No. I mean yes." I remember then about not having any money. "A glass of water. Please."

She eyes me up and down. "That's it?"

"Yes. Thanks," I say. She turns around. "Sorry," I say to her back.

She's back in a minute with the water. "Thanks," I say. But she's gone again, putting a gigantic coffee filter inside a gigantic coffee machine, then waiting on a businessman who wants a large black coffee to go.

I sip my water slowly, trying to make it last. I make a conscious effort to stop shivering; it doesn't work. Peggy keeps looking over at me; I do my best to act like I don't notice. She wipes down the counter with a rag. I wrap my arms around myself. Out of the corner of my eye I see her nod, like she's just decided something important. She flips a switch on a big machine on the counter; it drones to life.

Then Peggy's standing in front of me with a cup of hot chocolate with a fancy, twirly peak of whipped cream on top.

"This is what you want, I think," she says. She puts another cup on the counter in front of me, splashes some coffee in it, takes a sip, swallows. She takes another sip. "Runaway?"

I wonder then if she's going to call the police. Or if anyone else from Sick Minds has ever ended up in here. And if they got kicked out. Or sent to Humdinger.

"Sort of," I say.

She exhales, the way Sydney does when she's blowing smoke rings.

"How could you tell?" I say.

She tips her chin up. "No coat. It's a little cold out there to be going around without a coat." She smiles. "I figured maybe you left somewhere in a hurry."

I cup my hands around the hot chocolate, hoping the warmth from the cup will pass through to my hands.

"Where you headed?" Peggy says.

"Nowhere. Home, I guess." I shrug and stare at the tray of cream-filleds.

"You want one of those?" she says.

"That's OK," I say. Then, "I don't have any money."

She whisks a sheet of waxed paper out of a little box, grabs a cream-filled, and puts it on a plate in front of me. "On the house," she says. The front door opens and a family comes in. Peggy helps them pick out a dozen to go. The men down the counter pay their bill and more people come and go while I eat my doughnut and drink my hot chocolate.

Peggy comes back, takes a sip of her coffee, and scrunches up her nose. "Cold," she says, sticking out her tongue. She studies me. "Anyone know where you are?"

"My dad. He's on his way."

She nods, evidently satisfied; I feel a little proud and a little embarrassed at the same time.

"Listen," Peggy says. "I got a kid. He's grown now. But he's still my baby, you understand?"

She says this with such certainty, I can only say yes, even though I'm not sure I do understand.

"He still lets me fuss over him, like when he was little." She beams. "When your dad gets here, he's probably gonna wanna fuss over you." She sips her coffee. "Let him."

I'm still not warmed up, not even after my second cup of hot chocolate, when I see the reflection of a familiar white car in the window. The car rocks to a halt and my dad jumps out,

142

taking three long, running strides to the door. He's not wearing a coat and the wind is blowing his hair up in wisps around his head.

Then he's inside the Dunkin' Donuts and I'm inside a warm, dark hug, a hug that smells like aftershave and spray starch and home. His whole body is shaking, but finally I'm not shaking anymore.

When he eventually draws away from me, he looks shy. He glances down and pats his pockets like he's looking for something, and I notice that his hair has thinned a little more on top. When he looks up again, his eyes are moist; my heart hurts.

He spins the vinyl stool next to me. "Mind if I join you?"

"Yes. I mean no. I don't mind."

He sits down cautiously, as if he's worried the stool is too small for him or something. He looks so tired and disheveled, his hair all mussed up like he's just woken up, I feel shy now, embarrassed for bothering him.

"You OK?" he says finally.

"I guess." I shrug.

The moment seems to call for a better answer, or at least a longer one. "Yeah, actually, I think I'm getting better. That's what's weird."

Peggy arrives with her coffee pot, my dad says yes please, and she pours some coffee into a mug in front of him. She gives him an appraising look, and I bob my head, wanting to tell her this is him, this is my dad. She half smiles, then pivots and goes off to wait on someone else.

My dad and I sip from our mugs and stare straight ahead at the racks of doughnuts. The wall across from us is covered with a mirror with pink writing, advertising different doughnut and coffee combinations, and between the letters I can see the two of us as we sip from our mugs, then set them on the counter at the same time. I watch my dad bite his lip, then I see myself in the mirror doing the same thing.

"I called that place, the place where you were, and told them you were safe," he says.

I nod a sort of thank-you.

"So," he says. "You went out for a jog?" His face goes from joking to serious.

I nod.

"Felt trapped?"

I want to agree because I think that's the answer he wants. But I can't say yes, since that's not why I left. I shrug.

There's a long silence, then we both start talking at the same time.

"You go ahead," he says.

"How's Sam?" I say.

"Sam? He's good. Really good." He sounds like he's trying to convince me, or maybe convince himself. "He hit 60 last week. Pounds."

"That's great," I say, thinking about how happy we all were when Tara weighed in at 99 last week.

"Yeah," he says. "Great, huh?" He still looks so tired and worried, though, I want to tell him something to cheer him up. I want to tell him everything I've learned at Sick

144

Minds. So he knows I'm OK, so he doesn't have to worry about me.

"You know," I say, in a very sane, you-won't-believe-this tone of voice, "I thought it was my fault. About Sam."

He glances over quickly, then away.

"I thought it was my fault, Sam getting sick."

He looks at me again, this time like he's seeing me for the first time.

"*I* was supposed to be watching him that day," he says to his coffee cup.

"I know," I say.

Something inside me loosens, because I really do know.

I set my cup on the counter, but it feels like I've just laid down something enormous, something very heavy.

I look over at my dad's profile. A muscle in his jaw is working the way Debbie's does when she's trying not to cry. He looks so miserable, I want to say something to make it all better.

"It's OK."

"No," he says. "It's not OK."

"No, really," I insist. "Don't worry. You have enough to worry about with Sam and Mom."

"Is that how it seems to you?"

"Yeah, I guess. Sometimes."

He runs his fingers through his hair, not making any real improvement. I trace a line in the powdered sugar on my plate.

"Well, I am. You know, worried about you. Now."

"I'm OK," I say. It's almost worse, him being worried. But I like it, too, a little.

Peggy doesn't want us to pay, but my dad insists, and then says we'll also take a dozen doughnuts to go. As we're standing at the cash register picking out two of this kind, two of that, I whisper that he should leave Peggy a big tip. He gives me a couple of dollars and I walk back to where we were sitting and tuck them under my hot chocolate mug.

She thanks us and my dad reaches across the counter and shakes her hand. She doesn't act like this is dorky, so I decide to shake her hand too. Then she goes off to wait on a couple of punk rockers.

"You wait here," my dad says. "I'll get the car warmed up, then you can come out."

"Sure," I say. "OK."

After a few minutes he comes back and says the car's all warmed up; he looks ridiculously happy about this. I look for Peggy so she can see how I'm following her advice, but she must be in the kitchen. My dad holds the door for me as we leave Dunkin' Donuts and he opens the car door for me when we get to the parking lot. I think about how normal we look compared to the punk rockers inside eating doughnuts; we must look like an old-time dad and daughter from some black-and-white TV show, but I don't care. I actually sort of like it.

He puts the car in reverse but keeps his foot on the brake. "So," he says. "Where're we going?"

This hadn't occurred to me — the idea that there's a next step. And that it's up to me to decide what that next step is.

"Home?" my dad says.

I picture my mom and Sam sitting in the breakfast nook, tatting and sorting, Linus outside chasing a squirrel. Then I imagine Sydney blowing smoke rings on the porch. Tara inviting me to play Ping-Pong. And the circle of feet in Group the day I cried. I picture Ruby's white nurse's shoes. And your little fabric shoes.

I shake my head.

"Back to Sick Minds," I say.

"What?" he says.

"That's what we call it. Sick Minds. Instead of Sea Pines."

"Oh." He takes this in, then smiles. "You sure?"

I wonder for a minute if I am sure. Then I know I am. "Uh huh," I say. "For a while."

He makes his *tkk, tkk* thinking sound, then nods. "OK," he says. He takes his foot off the brake and we pull out of the parking lot.

We cross the highway and swing past the pay phone where the operator helped me call collect. Then the businesses on the highway glide by, one by one. The carpet store with its loud sale signs. A video rental place. A Burger King, a Dairy Queen. I realize in an instant that the trip back to Sick Minds will be much faster than the trip away from it. "Could you go a little slower?" I say.

He doesn't answer, doesn't ask why, he just does what I ask.

I want to use every minute talking. But it's my dad who says something first.

"I'm, uh, sorry I never came and saw you there." He says this quietly, glancing over at me, then back at the road.

"It's OK," I say.

"Will you quit saying that?" he says. "It's not OK."

"OK," I say. Then, "Actually, I've got a lot of repressed hostility about it."

He looks startled, then I laugh and he laughs and I offer a silent thank-you to Amanda, who couldn't possibly know how she helped me.

"At least you brought Mom and Sam to visiting day," I say.

"Where'd you get that idea?"

"I don't know. I just figured . . ."

"Well, I didn't."

He checks the rearview mirror, changes lanes, comes back to the conversation.

"She drove herself," he says.

"Really?"

"Really."

I imagine my mom driving, achingly slowly, her and Sam strapped in their seat belts, my mom leaning forward, her hands gripping the steering wheel.

"Wow," is all I can say.

A band of light, the reflection from the rearview mirror, shines across my dad's features.

"Things are . . . . a little different now," he says haltingly.

"What do you mean?"

"After you . . . left, you know, for . . . what do you call it? Sick Minds?"

I grin; this sounds funny coming from my dad.

"We're trying harder now," he says. "Your mom and me. I, um, I'm trying to be around more."

I can't quite picture him at the breakfast nook while my mom tats and Sam sorts, but I want to believe him, because he seems to need me to believe.

We're at a stoplight. My dad looks over at me, studying my face. A horn beeps behind us. My dad checks the rearview mirror again, startled, as if he's forgotten we're on a busy road.

• • •

When we pull up to the entrance of Sick Minds, I ask my dad if we can drive around the block once before we go in. He takes his foot off the gas and lets the car glide past. We drive slowly by a few scattered houses, then turn the corner and inch past a housing development.

I clutch the box of doughnuts to my stomach and imagine what it'll be like to see everybody again. The dashboard clock says 7:12. It's only a few hours since I left, even though it feels like it's been days. At 7:12, everyone will be in evening Study Hall. Sydney and Tara and Debbie. Even Amanda. Ruby will be patrolling the halls in her squeaky shoes. And suddenly I want to be back there. Right away.

"It's OK," I say to my dad. "We can go in now."

• • •

I sit in the waiting room outside Mrs. Bryant's office, the box of doughnuts still in my lap, while my dad goes in and explains. On the way in from the parking lot I told him I was afraid they'd send me to Humdinger or maybe even kick me out. "Let me handle it," he said. I remembered Peggy's advice and decided to go ahead and let him be the dad and me just be the kid.

When he comes out with Mrs. Bryant, I notice that his hair is still a mess from being outside in the wind; I have an urge to fix it for him, get a comb and make it all neat again, but I can tell from the look on Mrs. Bryant's face that I have bigger things to worry about.

"You had us worried," she says, after we all sit down.

"I'm sorry." I know this is the good-manners thing to say.

"Well." A sort of smile passes over her face. "I'm glad you came back."

"*Me too.*" I mean this, suddenly, with all my heart.

They look at me like they don't quite understand and I try hard to find the words that will make them see what I mean. "I . . . I want . . . I want . . ." And then I know what it is I wanted so badly the day Tiffany went home, the day it first felt like spring, when I pictured kids riding bikes, dads cooking on grills, moms making lemonade. "I want to get better."

My dad starts patting his pockets like he's looking for something. But I know he's just trying to do something so he doesn't cry. I smile at him because I know this isn't something to cry about.

150

My dad and Mrs. Bryant are talking about dates, insurance policies, adult stuff. But all I can think about is how when I get back to the dorm wing, I'm going to see if it would be okay if I offer everyone a doughnut.

Then, tomorrow, I'm going down to your office first thing in the morning. And tell you everything.

More from
Patricia McCormick

On Writing Cut

I entered the locked ward with some trepidation. The girls on the other side of the door were all confined there because of dangerous things they'd done with sharp objects: shards of glass, box cutters, knives. Friends had questioned my decision to visit the ward. But these girls weren't dangerous to others: They were hurting themselves.

I was nervous because I'd written a manuscript about a girl who cut herself—and I'm not a cutter. I was sure the girls would call me out as phony, as a poser, as someone who'd exploited their pain. I'd spent more than two years working on the book—but I was prepared to toss it in the garbage if these girls told me that I had no right to try to tell their story.

One by one, they approached me. With curiosity, with a nervousness of their own. And one by one, they told me their stories. Stories of terrible violence, committed against themselves. But what moved me even more was the secrecy and isolation they suffered.

One girl, a pretty blonde with expressive blue eyes, told me she'd worn a turtleneck when she went to the beach with her family; no one asked why. Another girl, with an adorable boyish haircut and mischievous eyes, said she kept going to the same hardware store to get bigger blades, wishing that the man behind the counter would ask her what she was doing with them. And another girl described telling her parents transparent lies about her cuts—blaming them on the cat or "falling on a Coke bottle"—always hoping they'd see through her stories.

What I realized then was that they *wanted* to be found out. They were caught in a cycle of hurting themselves, then being terribly ashamed and afraid of what they'd done, feelings that would drive them to hurt themselves again—each time, a little worse. They were practically advertising what they were doing because they didn't know how to stop.

Some told friends—then begged their friends not to say anything. Those friends were pulled into the secret and struggled with their own guilt and worry. But a lot of the girls at S.A.F.E. (Self-Abuse Finally Ends) Alternatives, the center I visited, were there *because* of those friends. Friends who were willing to put their friendship on the line by telling a trusted adult, because they recognized that it was a secret too dangerous to keep.

Since *Cut* was published I've heard from thousands of readers: girls who say the book prompted them to get help; concerned friends and parents; teachers and therapists who want to understand a behavior that confuses and frightens them.

Most moving, though, were the comments from the girls in that locked ward. They all read my manuscript—then asked to see my scars. I told them, with some hesitation, that I made the story up, that I had never self-injured. "But you told *my* story," they each said. "How could you know how it felt?" And it dawned on me, then, finally, why I identified with them, why I'd written the book in the first place.

I *was* that girl in the book—the girl who was so lonely, so angry and hurt, and so confused, but I didn't have the words for it. I remember all too well how alone I felt. I did some self-destructive things—I think we all do—and took on responsibility and shame for things that weren't really mine to shoulder. The facts of my life were different from theirs; the emotional truth was the same.

The girls at S.A.F.E. Alternatives gave me their blessing to publish the book. In fact, they were really pleased to see that their experience—something cloaked in secrecy and shame—would be put into words. With their own recoveries underway, they hoped the book would lead others struggling with self-injury to feel less alone and get help. By giving Callie a voice, they said, the book was giving *them* a voice.

But it was those girls who gave me the biggest gift. They gave me the confidence to believe in the power of fiction to connect us more deeply, perhaps, than the facts ever could.

A Conversation with Patricia McCormick

Where did you grow up? What was it like?
I grew up in a rather bland suburban development, not unlike the setting in my book. It was a place that, perhaps because of the sameness of all the houses, often made me feel different, out of place, and lonely. In particular, there's a scene in the opening of *Cut* where the main character, Callie, is coming home in the dark and sees "houses with windows of square yellow light where the mothers were inside making dinner [and] houses with windows of square blue light where kids were inside watching TV." This is a memory straight out of my childhood from a lonely night when I was on the outside looking in on homes that seemed perfectly ordinary and therefore perfect.

Where did *Cut* come from?

I wish I knew. The easy answer is that it was inspired by reading about the phenomenon of girls cutting themselves in secret, something that both upset and fascinated me. The complicated answer, the one that even I didn't understand until I'd finished the book, was that I was unconsciously exploring my own self-sabotaging tendencies. I am not a cutter; I'm too much of a chicken to ever hurt myself with a blade. But I am, and I think we all are, self-destructive at times — usually at the very times we need to take the best care of ourselves. By writing *Cut*, I explored what prompted Callie, a sensitive fifteen-year-old girl not unlike me when I was fifteen, to hurt herself and feel so ashamed and desperate about it that she couldn't tell anyone. But, honestly, I didn't set out to investigate self-injury; the book just unfolded that way.

You mentioned that Callie is similar to you at fifteen years old. Can you tell us a bit about what high school was like for you?

I went to a Catholic high school and was a debate team nerd. I think we are similar in that we were both feeling isolated and out of place in a world where everybody else looked like they really had it together.

How much research did you do? Who were some of the people you talked to?

I started out reading everything I could about cutting, although at the time there wasn't much written and there

159

was only one young adult novel on the topic. Since I have a background as a reporter, I then planned to interview girls who self-injured and distill their stories into a fictional one. A very wise friend told me not to do that; she said that kind of factual material would get in the way of me, as a fiction writer, imagining what it would be like to be a cutter. I took her advice and am glad I did. As a result, the whole story comes from my imagination and from experiences I had visiting a friend who was in a place like Sea Pines, the rehab facility in the book. After I'd finished the first draft of the book, I went to S.A.F.E. Alternatives, an amazing facility that treats people who self-injure. I spent several days there absorbing everything I could about the place—the rooms, the girls, the staff, the schedule, the food—everything. To my great surprise and relief, almost every detail was exactly like those I'd imagined in my book! I am forever indebted to the girls at S.A.F.E., though, for sharing their stories with me. Without their trust I would never have had the confidence to believe that the story that I had imagined was so true and so worth telling.

What was the hardest part about writing *Cut*?
The hardest part was learning to really love the main character. For the longest time, I was standing apart from her —judging her, I think. Then, one day I was sitting on the subway and it dawned on me that I had to love her, I had to fully enter into her experience. And I had to be compassionate toward her in a way she wasn't being toward herself. Once I made that mental switch, everything changed.

Callie has a wonderful and fierce bond with Sam. Do you have any siblings of your own?

I have three younger sisters, including one who once had a traumatic allergic reaction to an asthma medication. She was a baby and I remember watching her skin actually turn blue; it was terrifying. She was the youngest and I was the oldest, and when our middle sisters developed a close bond, I think we both felt a little left out, so we made a pact to be buddies despite a ten-year age difference. One of the ways we always stayed close was via mail: I sent her a stick of gum one time, she sent me pictures of kittens. Maybe that's why Sam sends Callie his Wayne Gretzky.

Did you have a general idea of how *Cut* was going to end? While everything isn't magically better for Callie, it finishes on a surprisingly hopeful note.

I didn't really have an ending in mind. But once Callie walked past the unlocked exit and ran off, I knew she had to find her way back: back to her father and then back to Sick Minds. Dunkin' Donuts—the only place open in the middle of the night, a place I was sure was full of adventure—always occupied a romantic place in my imagination growing up. So it seemed only natural that's where Callie would end up.

Before you wrote *Cut* you were a journalist. What made you decide to write a novel for teens?

Teenagers are constantly in the act of becoming: becoming who they're going to be, becoming aware of the world. It's the most euphoric, most depressing, most exciting, most bewildering time of life and therefore I think the most interesting to write about.

What's it like to write for and about teens?
It is so exciting—thrilling, really—to be part of an imprint dedicated to speaking honestly and directly to teenage readers. Teenagers are, in my view, the most perceptive and open-minded readers there are; they are also the most underestimated group in the marketplace. The books that the people at PUSH aspire to publish are challenging, uncensored books for readers who are looking for something more. Another aspect of being part of PUSH that is unlike any other publishing experience is that PUSH is about new voices, about finding new talents and hearing directly from readers who send in their own work. My book is about one girl finding her voice, finding the courage to put her life into words. PUSH is about finding many new voices. The books I read as a teenager went straight to my heart; they were very influential in helping me figure who and what I wanted to be. To have the chance to communicate with other readers who are in the midst of that search is profoundly satisfying.

Who are your literary influences?
I love the work of Carolyn Coman, Kaye Gibbons, Russell Banks, and Tobias Wolff. What these writers have in common is that they treat the experience of adolescence and of growing up with great respect and compassion. I'm also very

lucky to count Rachel Cohn as one of my closest friends. No one gets teenagers—with all their longing, their humor, and their irreverence—like Rachel.

What are your cinematic influences?
I love to watch movies that are told from the point of view of a teenager, or even a younger adolescent, because those characters are often on the perimeter in real life. I think that the perspective of an outsider is the most interesting, perhaps because it's usually tinged with longing, or with cynicism, or with a poignant or slightly skewed quality that is way more interesting than a mainstream view. Off the top of my head, films that embody this slightly off-center view: *Welcome to the Dollhouse*, *This Boy's Life*, and *Girl, Interrupted*.

A person stops you on the street and asks you to tell him something cool. What do you say?
Possibly one of the coolest things I've ever done was to go rappelling off a cliff in the Blue Mountains of Australia. Wearing a harness and tethered to a rope staked in the top of the mountain, you lower yourself over the edge of a very sheer cliff and gradually walk down the face of the mountain until, eventually, the cliff face falls away and you descend through space as you slide down the rope. I was TERRIFIED to do this because, as I mentioned, I'm a big chicken, and because I have a huge fear of heights. But for some reason, I signed up for this adventure and simply did it. I felt unbelievably light when it was over, like I could do anything.

Why would I tell someone about it if they wanted to hear about something cool? What was cool was that I was terrified and I still did it. As someone once told me, it's not brave if you're not scared.

If you had to pick a quote to fit your life right now, what would it be?
A Thoreau quote taped to the front of my diary: "Go confidently in the direction of your dreams! Live the life you've imagined."

Writing. How do you go about it?
Having a routine is key for me. I'm also very lucky to have a place where I can write without the distractions of home, the phone, and the refrigerator: I go to a place in New York called The Writers Room. It's this absolutely serene place filled with desks occupied by other writers hard at work—screenwriters, poets, novelists, playwrights. All you hear is the gentle clicking of computer keys as you get lost in writing your stories. I try to go there four days a week and work from early morning till after lunch. I write without a plan or an outline because I find that that cramps my thinking. I discover what the book is about as I go along, which is kind of cool because it's like the reader's experience. I try to be fearless as I write, and I try to catch myself when I'm avoiding something difficult or writing stylishly because, at least for me, that's also a way of avoiding getting personal in my writing. I've always been pretty hard on myself as a critic

and editor—which I'm trying to stop since that attitude only hurts my confidence, which in turn shuts down creativity.

Do you have any superstitions or rituals when writing?
When the going gets rough, I eat M&M'S. When I want to reward myself for a good day's work, I eat M&M'S. It's all about the M&M'S.

A lot of your readers aspire to be writers as well. Any tips, hints, or advice for them?
My main advice: unplug. To be able to create, you need to develop a capacity for silence. If you're constantly receiving input—from a text, a screen, a pair of headphones—you are the recipient of someone *else's* creative output. That output crowds out what you can create. You'll be amazed at what your own imagination offers up when you tune out the fruits of someone else's imagination.

Who wrote the book of love?
Gosh. I don't know. Aren't we all writing it together every day?

Resources

The Cornell Research Program on Self-Injurious Behavior in Adolescents and Young Adults is a great resource for teachers and parents. Visit their website at *www.crpsib.com*.

S.A.F.E. Alternatives is the group whose facility Patricia McCormick visited. More information and resources can be found on their website: *www.selfinjury.com*.

Acknowledgments

I'm deeply grateful to The Writers Room, an oasis of serenity in downtown New York; to the Vermont College graduate program in writing for young people, which supported my work at a crucial juncture; to my friends Bridget Starr Taylor, Hallie Cohen, Annie Pleshette Murphy, Chris Riley, Joan Oziel, Joan Gillis, Meg Drislane, Anna An, and Cathy Bailey, who believed in this story even when I didn't; to Katya Rice, who copyedited with sensitivity and good cheer; to Carolyn Coman, the first person to call these pages a book; to Stephen Roxburgh, my editor and publisher; and most of all to my family, Paul, Meaghan, Matt, and Brandon, who have taught me so much about love and honesty.

About the Author

Patricia McCormick, a National Book Award finalist, is the author of four critically acclaimed novels: *Purple Heart*, a suspenseful psychological novel that explores the killing of a ten-year-old boy in Iraq; *Sold*, a deeply moving account of sexual trafficking; *My Brother's Keeper*, a realistic view of teenage substance abuse; and *Cut*, an intimate portrait of one girl's struggle with self-injury.

McCormick was named a New York Foundation on the Arts Fellow in 2004. She is also the winner of the 2009 German Peace Prize for Youth Literature.

She is a graduate of the Columbia University Graduate School of Journalism and lives in Manhattan.